# It was coming straight at them.

A truck rumbling down the road at breakneck speed.

"Run!" Tate yelled.

They took a dozen steps before gunshots exploded around them...and someone yelled, "Freeze!"

As Liberty halted, she felt Tate's arms encircle her. She didn't ever want to move. Not because she would be shot but because Tate's arms were around her. Strong arms she had missed so much it made her want to cry.

"Get in the truck," the gunman ordered. He zip-tied their wrists, so tight the strap cut off her circulation.

Kidnapped.

What was her boss going to think?

First he'd have to realize what happened to her. But then would he think she was part of this with Tate?

"What are you going to do with us?"

He tipped his head back and let out a roar of laughter. His cackle told her what she needed to know. He planned to kill them.

**Lisa Phillips** is a British-born tea-drinking, guitar-playing wife and mom of two. She and her husband lead worship together at their local church. Lisa pens high-stakes stories of mayhem and disaster where you can find made-for-each-other love that always ends in a happily-ever-after. She understands that faith is a work in progress more exciting than any story she can dream up. Lisa blogs monthly at teamloveontherun.com, and you can find out more about her books at authorlisaphillips.com.

## Books by Lisa Phillips

### Love Inspired Suspense

### Secret Service Agents

*Security Detail*
*Homefront Defenders*
*Yuletide Suspect*

*Double Agent*
*Star Witness*
*Manhunt*
*Easy Prey*
*Sudden Recall*
*Dead End*

# YULETIDE
# SUSPECT

## LISA PHILLIPS

**HARLEQUIN** LOVE INSPIRED SUSPENSE

Recycling programs
for this product may
not exist in your area.

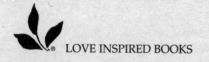

LOVE INSPIRED BOOKS

ISBN-13: 978-0-373-45751-9

Yuletide Suspect

Copyright © 2017 by Lisa Phillips

www.Harlequin.com

**Printed in U.S.A.**

And when he comes home, he calls together his friends and neighbors, saying to them, "Rejoice with me, for I have found my sheep, which was lost!"
*—Luke* 15:6

To all my readers.

Have a very merry and blessed Christmas season.

# ONE

Arrest him. Or apologize.

Liberty Westmark gripped the steering wheel, not sure which she was going to do first. If she ever got there. She peered out the windshield, where fat flakes of snow obscured both lanes of the highway beyond her high beams.

"In six hundred yards, turn right."

The voice of her GPS was loud and clear, but the way was not. She'd probably wind up turning into a ditch. It would serve her right to end up the sad conclusion of an obscure news article about the snowstorm of the century. Heartwarming. She rolled her eyes and muttered, "Lone Secret Service agent who left ahead of her team gets lost and freezes to death chasing a dream."

She froze. A *suspect*.

Not a dream.

Where had that come from, anyway? The fact that Tate Almers had been her fiancé a year ago was absolutely not relevant anymore—unless she got the chance to apologize. Otherwise this was just work, and once she had Tate in custody she could drop him off at the nearest federal agency office and go back to her cozy DC condo and her hairless cat.

Job done.

It was a courtesy, nothing more. Tate might have done something bad—really bad—but the qualifier was what made her unable to believe it was actually his doing. A plane had gone down, and three people were missing— two White House staffers and a senator. The man she had known and worked with—okay, and loved—would never have done something like this. That history was why she'd convinced the director she should come here ahead of the rest of the team.

Liberty was going to give Tate the courtesy of explaining, and then he could tell his former Secret Service team the same thing.

The turn came up faster than she was expecting. Liberty hit the brakes and took the corner too fast. The back end of her car hit ice and fishtailed. Stupid man, living in the middle of stupid nowhere. The car kept spinning. Liberty gripped the wheel harder, like it was going to help.

She squealed.

When the car came to a stop, she was sideways on the single-track road.

Liberty sighed. "No one heard that squeal."

She was still the fully fledged Secret Service agent her teammates respected. Just a little ice that threw her for a minute. No big deal. She was fine.

Liberty shook off the rush of adrenaline that had set her heart racing and righted the car on the road. A single lane, probably dirt or gravel, but right now it was covered in a layer of snow and ice. Liberty drove slower than she needed to down to the house.

It was more of a cabin, really. The roofline was lit up with Christmas lights, and she could see a Christmas tree in the front window, the only light in the house. Tears filled her eyes. It was beautiful, like a Christmas card. Tate was a no-nonsense kind of guy, and this was anything but. What on earth? Then it hit her. What if he was married now? What if he'd found someone else, and this was all for *her*?

Liberty nearly turned around and left, but the Secret Service would be here soon and she wanted answers. After it was done, she'd be able to move on for good. Sure, he might be married, but actually that was better. It would help sever those few lingering ties, right?

Liberty cracked the car door and braced against the cold as she got out, then leaned back in and grabbed her gloves. The wool wouldn't protect her much against this temperature. Cold cut through the layers of her clothing, and the wind chafed her cheeks. Her coat covered her badge, but maybe there would be time to really talk before she told him she was here for work reasons.

A couple of dogs barked, but not in the house. The sound came from the barn. Liberty waded through snow and banged her fist on the barn door. It swung open and two dogs raced toward her, barking louder. Liberty took a step back.

Tate stepped out of the barn, but she couldn't take her focus off the dogs, even as she backed up more across the stretch of snow over the driveway between the barn and the house. They barked and circled her, their attention imposing enough that Liberty didn't move.

"Good boys. Sit."

Both dogs sat, one on either side of her. Liberty wanted to slump onto the packed down snow between them. The sound of Tate's voice cut through her and left a ragged wound in its wake. She glanced up, and her eyes locked with his. It was too dark to get a good look, but in the glow of the Christmas lights the line of his jaw was set. He wasn't happy.

One of the dogs broke his sit and barked.

Tate's eyes widened, fixed on some point beyond her, away from the house. "What…" He lunged and grabbed her arm, dragged her the ten feet or so back toward the barn and yelled, "Bubblegum!"

A gunshot went off. Liberty ducked, having no idea where the shot had come from. She skidded on the barn floor, reached the end of Tate's grasp and snapped back toward him. She grimaced. Tate didn't let go. Outside the dogs barked, and someone yelled.

"Intruder," he said. "I thought it was you who set off the alarm, but there was a man out there with a gun." A gunshot went off outside. "Do you have your weapon?"

Liberty pulled her gun from the holster at her back, under her jacket. He grabbed it from her. "Hey—"

Tate stepped outside and shut the door behind him.

The dogs continued to bark. Outside, Tate yelled, "Hey!"

A gunshot followed.

Liberty pulled the backup weapon from her ankle holster and moved to the door. She was the Secret Service agent. Sure, Tate had been one, too, over a year ago. But he'd quit, and Liberty didn't have time to think through all of that—or the fact that it was basically her fault.

Liberty wanted to pray, but that part of her life was long gone, just like her love life. Neither had ever done her any favors or bettered her in any way. She'd given up on God and romance both in the last eighteen months.

This was one last favor to Tate, and then she was done. Liberty was going to live her life her way, on her terms.

The door swung open before she reached it. Tate strode to her, and the dogs raced in around him. Liberty shook her head. "What on earth was that? And why did you shut me in here?"

"Man outside," he said, without handing her weapon back to her. "An intruder, which I already mentioned." He didn't look happy. "He ran off. The dogs did their job."

As though they knew he'd complimented them, the two dogs returned to his side and sat to be petted. One was a German shepherd, lean enough that Liberty wanted to feed the animal treats. The other was a stocky Airedale who came to her next. She didn't pet him.

Tate raised his eyebrow. "You still have that ugly cat?"

She ignored the question. Loki was alive and well, not that it was any of his business. "Bubblegum?" They had to talk about something; otherwise she'd just stare at the blond hair sticking out the bottom of his knit beanie. His hair grew fast and had to be cut frequently, but it seemed Tate no longer cared. He wore the mountain man uniform of jeans and a checkered shirt under a padded denim jacket. No gloves. Wasn't he cold?

"Bubblegum is a command. If the person attacking you doesn't know what you just asked your dog to do, they'll think twice." Tate's jaw was hard again. "He shot at them, saw me and then ran off."

"Are you going to give me my gun back?"

Tate stood stunned for a second before he forced himself to snap out of it. He motioned for her to back up.

"You have one, and mine are all in the house. I'll be keeping this until I know for sure he's gone."

He had to focus on the intruder who'd just tried to kill him. Otherwise he'd stare at her blond hair. Those blue-green eyes. *Focus.*

"That is against policy and you know it." She used her most snooty voice, and it almost made him smile. Almost. "I can't lend out my duty weapon."

"I'll be sure to write that on the form I fill out explaining why you're dead." Tate swept past her and moved toward the door again. Liberty huffed behind him, but he figured she didn't argue because she knew he wasn't wrong.

Tate cracked open the door, peered out into the night and tried to tamp down the boiling rage. Shoot at him? Whatever. Shoot at his dogs? Unacceptable. Tate adjusted his grip on the gun, though using it would deny him the fight he was itching for. He'd always had a temper problem. He'd learned in the army how to channel it into discipline, and during his time with the Secret Service, Tate had rarely lost his cool. It never went well when he did.

He sucked in a breath of icy air and counted to ten in his head. One of the dog's muzzles touched his leg, and he reached down to pet Joey. His Airedale boy loved life and thought everything was a game. The German shepherd, Gem, was more task oriented. Wake up. Eat. Work. Sleep. Repeat.

"Looks clear."

He shoved the door wider and walked out. Snow was thick on the ground and falling fast. They'd have another two feet by tomorrow, but that wasn't what had his attention. He pointed at the far end of his front yard where the dense trees began. They blocked his view of the land, but he much preferred being in a cocoon of privacy.

Tate pointed. "That's where he ran off to."

"And you shoved me in the barn so you could take care of it?"

She was still stuck on that? "Guess it was a reflex. All those years of protection duty for the Secret Service ingrained in me. I'm the one who faces the danger."

"And the dogs."

She really was intent on arguing, wasn't she? Tate sighed. "They're trained."

"And I'm not? I'm still a Secret Service agent, Tate."

He turned to her. "That's not what I meant." Not that he'd have heard from out here if she'd quit or not.

He didn't know how to get himself out of this one, and why did he even feel like he needed to? He didn't owe her anything, and he didn't want her to owe him anything back. Whatever they'd had was done now. She'd killed it when she gave him his ring back and sent him packing.

Tate had lost it a couple of days later and gotten pushed into early retirement from the Secret Service over it, but this life was better. Simpler. He knew who he was out here, with the dogs.

Tate scanned the area but couldn't see any sign of the gunman. The man might return. He could scout out the area and see if the guy was still here, but he'd have to do it after Liberty left.

The dogs trotted along. Gem scanned the area, but Joey ran in circles, ready to play. Tate motioned with his hand and gave them the command to head for the porch and wait for him there. He used it mostly when the UPS guy delivered packages, but it came in handy at other times as well.

Tate didn't even want to contemplate what it meant that Liberty was here. He'd do so later, when he was alone again. The way he preferred it.

*Liar.*

Okay, so it wasn't his choice, but life was life. She'd broken up with him. Called off the whole thing, and he didn't even know why, so he'd simply concluded it was him. He'd always known there was something defective in him, and she'd tried to make it work. Until she realized it never would.

Tate stopped beside her car and opened the driver's-side door. Waited. She didn't move, just stood there looking like she had so much to say. He really didn't want to hear any of it. What was the point? He took her in. All her blond hair, even softer than it looked, was secured back in a business ponytail. Dress slacks. Completely the wrong shoes to be traipsing around in snow. The bottom few inches of her pants were wet, but it wasn't his problem, now was it? Not anymore.

Liberty's eyebrows pinched together. She wore makeup, but not much. The top curve of her lip had a bump he'd always thought was adorable, as she'd been born with a cleft palate. The scar where it had been repaired was barely visible now. Still cute, though.

"We should call the police and report that man. He tried to kill you."

Tate said, "Maybe he was here to kill *you*."

Liberty blinked. "I… No, I don't think so." Still, there was a question in her eyes as she considered it.

Tate didn't want to think about her being in danger. It was a reality of being a Secret Service agent, but not one he was going to dwell on. "He can't have known you'd be here, unless he followed you, and how could he do it through this terrain, on foot?" Only her car was out here. His truck was under the carport.

Liberty pulled out her phone. "I'll call emergency services. Get a sheriff, or whoever is the law around here, to come over."

"Give me your phone. I'll call him." Even if her cell actually worked up here, she shouldn't do the talking. That was more involvement than she needed to have in this situation.

Then again, if she left now, he could make the report to the sheriff and perhaps pretend she'd never even been here. It wasn't exactly honest, but tell that to his heart.

Liberty clutched the phone. "I've given you enough already."

She had no idea. "I don't have a signal, and I don't have a landline either."

"So how do you communicate with people?"

Tate said, "Shortwave radio."

Liberty glanced up from her phone. Evidently she had the one carrier that actually got a signal up here. "There's no reason to be rude."

She thought he was lying? Tate just enjoyed his privacy.

She said, "I know you want me to leave, but there's a reason I'm here, so I'm not going to go. I came to tell you the Secret Service is on their way here to talk with you."

"About what?" He had even less to say to his former employer than he did to his former fiancée.

"A plane went missing a hundred miles from here. Two White House staffers and a senator were on board."

"I haven't heard anything about it." Not that he watched the news much. His aerial only got half a dozen channels, and he didn't listen to the police band all the time on his scanner.

She kept talking. "It happened in the early hours of this morning. They lost contact right after the pilot sent out a distress call. We don't know if the plane went down or if they were hijacked. Everyone is out looking for it."

"I'm sure I can lend some assistance with the search," he said. "For old times' sake."

"That isn't why the Secret Service wants to talk with you."

Tate didn't know what else there would be to say. It didn't seem like this had anything to do with him. "They'll have to get in line. I need to make a report with the sheriff about a gunman on my property."

Liberty let him change the subject. "Did you see who it was?"

Tate shook his head, still leaning his forearms on her open car door. Was she ever going to get in and drive away? This was painful enough without her drawing it out.

Tate sighed. "I didn't get a good look at his face, but he didn't seem familiar to me." And it had definitely been a man. "Joey nearly chased him to the trees."

Liberty didn't smile. He knew she liked dogs, so he figured the problem was him. Tate glanced at the dogs. Joey wasn't sitting the way Gem was. Instead, the Airedale paced the porch by the front door with his nose to the mat. He pawed at the door and then barked once.

Tate saw the flash of movement through the living room window.

He started running toward his cabin. "Someone's in the house."

# TWO

Tate ran to the front door, so Liberty circled the house in case the intruder ran out the back. It was slow going, wading through thick snow, but she was already soaked and there would be time later to thaw out her toes. Liberty pulled out her cell phone and dialed emergency services. She requested the police, and was told the sheriff was on his way. The dispatcher seemed to know exactly where Tate's house was, but this was a small town. Maybe they knew each other. Maybe she—it had been a woman—was his girlfriend.

Liberty stuffed her phone back in her jacket pocket and huffed out a breath at the workout she was getting. Okay, not only at the workout. Who cared if there was someone in Tate's life now? It wasn't like she had any claim on him. Not since she'd broken it off and severed the tie between them. As much as it had pained her to do it—and the reason for it hurt almost more than the act of doing it—Liberty hadn't had another choice.

There was no future for them.

Still, if she got the chance, then she might tell him she regretted hurting him. But Liberty was never, ever going to tell him why. She could barely even think about it herself.

She reached the rear corner of the cabin, and the back door slammed. Liberty brought her gun up as the man flew out the door, stumbled and then started to run.

"Secret Service! Freeze!" Her voice barely carried.

He didn't even slow down.

She ran after him. Tate rushed out the back door and got to the man first, launched himself at the guy and tackled his legs. The two went down in the snow like an ugly version of a snow angel. Tate grunted, and the two men struggled.

Liberty stopped six feet away and planted her now-numb feet. "Freeze, or I'll shoot!" Tate would have to get out of the way first, but the man didn't know.

Tate shifted and she saw the man's face. He was probably in his midthirties.

He gritted his teeth and struggled. Tate jammed his arm up under the man's chin. "Who are you?"

The man jerked his head around, trying to get away. "Get off me." His gaze found hers, and she saw the moment he realized he'd lost this fight to the two of them. His eyes flashed. "Let me go."

If he was going to try to get her to shoot him, Liberty wasn't going to oblige. Suicide by cop might be something the police had to face, but it wasn't part of her résumé. "Tate."

He lifted the man off the snow to his feet. "Who are you?"

The guy looked like he was about to bolt. He wore jeans, boots and a heavy jacket. The men had both dressed for the weather, while Liberty was dressed for a mild winter in DC. Which was exactly what they'd been having. How was she to know this part of Montana was freezing and buried under four feet of snow?

When the man didn't answer, Tate said, "Find me something to secure him with."

Liberty went inside and found a dog leash hanging by the front door, beside where a big duffel sat on the floor. He'd always carried a bag to his workouts. The two animals were on dog beds in the living room, making the Christmas picture complete. They watched her move through the cabin, but thankfully didn't come over expecting her to pet them. Liberty couldn't handle that, when they would only remind her of her favorite dog. She'd had only cats since Beauregard died.

Hurrying back to Tate, Liberty held out the leash. He motioned to the guy with a tilt of his head. "You do it."

"Put your hands behind your back." She stowed her weapon and stepped behind him, where she secured his hands with the leash. "The sheriff is on his way."

"Good." Tate tugged on the man's elbow, took him into the kitchen and deposited the man on a chair. "Don't move."

Liberty shut the back door and took off her gloves, so thin they were pointless. She blew on one hand, then the other, switching off the hand holding her gun as she attempted to impart some warmth back in her stiff fingers. Tate frowned and then hit the power icon on the display of his coffee maker. Fancy. She used a four-cup coffeepot, the cheapest she could find, but he'd always been particular about what brand he drank. Liberty didn't care, so long as it was thick, hot and strong.

The man in the chair glanced between them but didn't say anything. Under the LED kitchen lights his clothes looked worn, his hair matted to the top of his head.

Liberty disliked silence. She motioned to the man but asked Tate, "Is this the guy from outside the barn?" He could have come back and gotten inside somehow. Though he'd had a gun before.

Tate shook his head. "This is a different guy." He pushed off the counter and took a step toward the man. "Come here with your partner. Come here to kill me. Why? Who am I to you?"

The guy looked away. Liberty had to wonder where the other man had disappeared to. Two assailants at Tate's house tonight, within minutes of each other? It seemed impossible they weren't connected.

Tate slammed both palms on his table. Liberty started and the seated man's eyes widened. Tate said, "Why did you come here to kill me?"

"I want my lawyer."

Liberty said, "We're not cops."

The minute the words were out of her mouth, Tate glanced at her. What? What had she said? He was being hard on the man. Yes, he had a right to be angry. But it was as though he'd forgotten everything they'd learned about questioning and just gone with what was in his gut: anger.

The last time she'd seen him, Tate had been so angry it had taken two of their fellow agents to pull him back from punching the director. He hadn't been fired; it'd been more like a mutual decision between both parties that he should move on from the Secret Service. Liberty's heart had broken even more than it already was that day, as she'd realized it was all her fault. Those tendencies he'd had as a kid to get mad instead of working through his problems had resurfaced through no fault of his own. Only hers.

Liberty strode to the intruder, because if she didn't she'd start crying, thinking about how everything between her and Tate had gone wrong. She didn't want to contemplate *again* how it was all her fault.

She said, "Stand up," and glanced at Tate. He nodded to indicate he had her back. Liberty stowed her gun, but the man hadn't moved. She hauled him up by his elbow and patted his pockets.

She found a cell phone, then a knife, and laid both on the table. She kept searching but found nothing else. Liberty grabbed the phone and stepped back. It wasn't locked, and it had no apps downloaded. There were no contacts listed, and if there were any messages, those had been deleted as well.

"It's clean." She tossed the phone on the table.

"Our friend here can talk to the sheriff."

"And it doesn't bother you that *his* friend tried to kill you?" She couldn't believe he was acting so blasé about this.

Tate shrugged. Was this his default now, when he'd decided he wasn't mad? The indifference almost hurt more than the anger.

One of the dogs started barking. Tate said, "Sheriff's here."

Liberty left him with the intruder and went to the front door.

Tate waited where he was until Liberty walked back in with the sheriff. He lifted his chin at Dane Winters, a good friend since peewee football. "This guy is all yours." Tate explained what had happened. The more he talked, the wider Dane's eyes grew.

"And you have a guest." Dane smiled. Because, yes,

Tate had shared about Liberty. But Dane could fish all he wanted, Tate wasn't going to spill.

"She was just leaving." His only guest except Dane in months.

He pushed off the counter and didn't offer anyone a cup of coffee, even though it was done brewing. He could drink it later and stay up all night brooding about the mess his life was now.

"Don't you want to know why I'm here?" Liberty asked.

She might think he should be curious about this missing plane. She likely would be if things were reversed and he'd shown up at her house after so long. They'd been engaged. Tate had honestly figured it meant something, but apparently not. It was a good thing she wasn't here for a reunion, or she would have been sorely disappointed.

Liberty looked almost sad. "Like I said, I'm here because a small aircraft, a business jet, went down not far from here. On board was a senator from Oklahoma and two White House staffers. Twelve hours ago we lost contact with them. We think the plane might've crashed somewhere close to here, and it's believed there was foul play involved, possibly with the pilot. At least, as much was indicated from the last radio call before communication was cut off." She paused. "We need to find those people."

"That should be an FBI investigation, shouldn't it?"

"They're on it. But at the top of the list of suspects who might be involved is a certain former Secret Service agent I happen to know personally. So I figured, why not? For old times' sake I'll visit this former agent and let him know the Secret Service and the FBI are all on their way here to ask you a whole lot of uncomfortable questions you aren't going to want to answer."

She couldn't seriously think he might be part of it. "You think I have something to hide? Something to do with this?"

"Do you?" She lifted her chin, like there was no history between them and she had every right to suspect him of something heinous. "It's a valid question."

"You really think I've changed that much?"

She didn't answer. Instead, she said, "The FBI and the Secret Service want to know if you're involved. But they're betting on the fact that a disgruntled former Secret Service agent—"

"Disgruntled?" Why would they think he harbored resentment? Tate had moved on. Wasn't it obvious?

Liberty shrugged. "Despite the cute cabin all decorated for a family Christmas, there is evidence against you. Seems to me from the blog, at least, that in the last few months your attitude has deteriorated. And it's the basis of their evidence."

"What blog?"

The sheriff shifted, but Dane couldn't hide the fact that he was listening to their conversation. They were friends, and Dane was curious. Tate didn't fault him for it. Even beyond this missing plane, there was a lot to talk about. Too bad there wasn't time.

And good thing he didn't want to talk about it anyway. His life now was none of her business.

Except the blog thing. What was that about?

When the sheriff peered at a tattoo on the man's neck—one Tate hadn't noticed until now—Tate went over to look as well. They glanced at each other, and Tate said, "Russians."

"Like the mob?" Liberty asked. "In backwoods Montana?"

The sheriff stepped back and shrugged. "It happens. Not often, but all kinds of people travel through this town on the way to somewhere. Some of them even like it and stay, and not all are law-abiding citizens." He glanced at Tate. "I got an update about this missing plane an hour ago. We should talk about it."

Tate didn't like the look on Dane's face at all. He'd known, and he stood there and let Liberty give her whole speech about him being a criminal.

"You want to take my badge for being involved, and keep it until I'm out from under suspicion?" The idea of losing the job as well, when he'd already lost so much, sat like a bad burrito in his stomach.

Liberty gasped. "His badge?"

He nearly kicked himself for saying it while she was here.

Dane said, "Tate is a deputy with the county sheriff's department. He only works shifts occasionally, and I pay him so much less than he's worth it's not even funny. But technically he's an employee. And as a sounding board, he's been invaluable."

Tate shook his head and pulled the badge from his drawer. "More like it's your attempt to make sure I'm not cooped up here all the time. Like it's a bad thing."

The sheriff shrugged again, pocketed the badge and then took the now-cuffed intruder out to his car where he'd be secure.

Liberty nodded. "The FBI doesn't know you're a deputy sheriff. It will strengthen our argument."

Tate said, "We don't have an argument, Liberty. We don't have anything. You took care of that." He saw the blow the words inflicted, but couldn't let himself care about it. She'd ripped him to shreds when she'd given his ring back and started the cascading fall of his life into this pit. A pit he tried to pretty up, just so he didn't dwell on the fact that it was kind of pathetic.

Now the Secret Service was here investigating a missing plane and three people, and they thought he was involved? He needed to get out in front of this, or he could wind up spending the rest of his life in prison for a crime he didn't commit.

If he cared enough, he'd ask her about the blog she'd mentioned. But Tate figured he'd find out soon enough. After she left his house.

He opened the hall closet and started to put his coat on.

Liberty had followed. "You're going out now?"

He looked at her, trying hard to hide everything he was feeling. "Lock the door before you leave."

"Where are you even going? You should stay here, help me convince the FBI you had nothing to do with this."

"Or I could go and find the plane and those missing people instead."

The sheriff walked back in. "If they think you're involved with this, it's going to be messy to unravel. But I'll do what I can. I've got your back, Tate. You know that."

He held out his hand, and Tate shook it.

Liberty didn't wait long before she asked, "Where are you going to look? Do you have an idea of where it might be?"

"Maybe." Tate pulled on a pair of gloves. "I know where I'm going to look first, at least." He turned away from their huddle toward the door. Yeah, this likely wasn't turning out the way she'd thought it would, but at least if he was gone looking for the plane, then the Secret Service might be convinced he wasn't involved.

Dane followed Tate to the door. Liberty walked over, her hand out for the sheriff to shake, but Dane didn't see it. His attention was on a black duffel leaned against the wall. The sheriff stepped toward the bag. "What is this?"

They worked out together, and Dane had never seen that bag before…because Tate had never seen that bag before. "It's not mine."

The bag was partially unzipped. The sheriff pulled the zipper back all the way as Liberty moved closer to them. Inside the duffel were bundles of cash secured by rubber bands, and an orange box the size of a lockbox like the one he kept his gun in. The sheriff lifted it out of the bag.

On the side of the box it said, FLIGHT RECORDER. DO NOT OPEN.

# THREE

"That's not mine." Tate said the words before he'd even thought them through.

The sheriff glanced over his shoulder at Tate, looking like he wanted to kick him. "Of course I know this isn't yours, dude. Except now what we have are two Russian intruders—one in my car, one who's fled—and a bag of money, along with what I'm guessing is the voice recorder for the plane that's currently missing. Which means any search the FBI has going for this thing—if it's active—is going to lead them right here. To the home of their lead suspect."

Liberty paled. "He's being framed."

Tate almost thought she might have cared for him just then as he studied her face and heard the soft tone of her words. Too bad he knew that wasn't the case. He didn't believe she'd come here because of any lingering feelings for him. She probably just wanted to save her reputation at work by convincing everyone she was prepared to do her job and arrest Tate—who was about to be labeled a traitor to his country.

Liberty looked at him, saw he was staring at her and glanced away.

"You should get your coat on," he said. Like he was going to hang around here so she could arrest him? She'd said the Secret Service were on their way. "And you should also switch out your shoes for boots."

Tate didn't wait around for her to comply. He strode to the closet and pulled out another set of gloves that would actually keep her hands warm, along with a hat, and turned back to her in time to see her plant one hand on her hip.

"What do you mean put my coat on? Why do I need my coat?"

"Because you're coming with me." He put all the outerwear in her hands and then turned to the sheriff. "You're good, right? I can leave?"

"Sure," Dane said with a distinct smirk on his face. "Just keep your phone on you."

"Good idea." Who knew how far away the plane was.

Tate strode to the kitchen and opened the junk drawer, not worried anyone would be able to use the thing to track him. It was almost useless, capable of making calls and sending texts—not that he ever did—and that was all.

He pulled out his cell phone and pressed the power button. Hopefully he'd charged it before he turned it off last time. He only kept it with him when he was on shift as a deputy sheriff. There was no signal on this mountain, so there was no point in having it on up here. One of these days he would switch to the carrier that actually got a tiny signal in this area, but he hadn't done it yet.

Tate slid the phone into his front pocket and found the keys to the snowmobile. He wasn't about to hang around and have this whole thing pinned on him. Not when he might be able to find the plane and prove his innocence. He'd have to deal with Liberty being with him—as opposed to somewhere else, probably causing trouble for him.

She wouldn't be causing him trouble on purpose, but she would have to do her job, and that wouldn't be good for him. If she was with Tate, he could keep an eye on her. And keep her safe in case that man had been here to hurt *her.*

The thoughts spun in his head like a tornado.

"Are you going to tell me where we're going?" Liberty asked.

"To find the plane," Tate said. Like that wasn't perfectly obvious. "If the Russian mob, or whoever is sitting in the back of the sheriff's car, is trying to frame me for this, then I'm not about to stay here and try to convince the feds and the Secret Service that I'm not involved." He'd burned those bridges to the ground when he'd tried to punch Locke his last day on the job. "There's no way I'm going to trust them to believe me when I can prove I'm innocent myself."

Locke had known exactly why Tate lost his cool and hadn't blamed him one bit. Which only made the whole situation all the more infuriating. His anger needed an outlet. It wasn't good if he bottled it up, so he had to channel it somewhere. There wasn't much to get mad about on this mountain, so he'd been fine.

Until Liberty showed up.

Now he wanted to kick a wall, because prison would *not* be good for him.

He trailed to his bedroom and got his Beretta from the safe. Two extra clips. He dropped them in a backpack as he walked to the entryway, where he handed it to Liberty. She'd need to carry it.

She raised her brows at his offering. "Is there a reason I have to come?"

Tate figured it was probably a valid question. Apparently Liberty was all about questions these days. The truth was he'd kind of missed her, which was totally messed up. But he had loved her, and she'd thrown it away. Maybe he didn't want to pass up this opportunity to hang out with her, even under the circumstances.

Instead of actually telling her, Tate waved toward the window. "Have you seen the weather out here? You don't go out in that alone. You take a buddy."

Tate thought he might have heard the sheriff snort, but he ignored it. Dane had figured out what it was about even if Liberty hadn't. She would eventually, and then he would be done for. She'd never liked being tricked.

Tate opened the door, stepped outside and headed for the shed. Joey barked and raced out into the snow behind him, ready for whatever adventure they were going on.

Tate turned to the house and called for Joey to follow him back inside. The dog bounded up the porch steps where Liberty stood, while Tate stayed at the bottom. Liberty jumped aside at the last minute, a nervous look on her face. Was she scared of dogs? He hadn't thought so. Hadn't she had a dog once? It was possible something had happened recently that he didn't know about. Tate figured it was just another indication of their incompatibility.

"You still have that ugly cat?"

Liberty's mouth dropped open. "Yes. You've already asked me that, Tate."

The sheriff stepped out with them and shut the door, almost choking in an attempt to hide his laughter. "I'll wait for the Secret Service and then take that guy in." He motioned to his car, where the intruder sat.

Liberty walked down the porch steps after Tate. "Just answer one question before we go find the plane."

Tate waited.

"What is up with the Christmas decorations? Your house looks like a postcard."

"It was a wreck, so I fixed it up. The Realtor's coming by first thing tomorrow morning for a showing."

She looked like he'd kicked her ugly bald cat.

Tate flicked two fingers toward the sheriff, who drove away with the intruder, and then stepped into the dark of the shed. He fired up the snowmobile and drove it out. Liberty walked over on black boots. She gaped. Tate just ignored it and said, "Get on. We've got a plane to find."

That got her moving. She jumped on behind him and set her hands on his shoulders. Tate reached back and pulled her arms around him. Before the feeling of her being so close could take root, he set off. Liberty squealed and held on tighter. She would get the hang of it pretty soon, and until then he would ignore the fact that she was holding on to him for dear life.

Tate found the path through the trees and headed up the mountain, toward the valley to the west of town. The snow was a thick covering, but the temperature wasn't too bad. He'd been out in colder weather than this, when the wind beat against him and he'd felt like he was frozen down to his bones.

As he drove, he prayed they would find the plane and the missing people—and that when this was done and Liberty went home, his heart would still be intact.

Four miles later her grip on his waist began to loosen. Half a mile after that she started to slide to the side. Tate shook his head. She'd fallen asleep, probably exhausted from a day of travel and then showing up at his house only to face intruders. Tate slowed the snowmobile to a stop and left it to idle while he reached back and shifted Liberty so she was sitting upright.

She looked even paler in the moonlight. He held her with one arm and then put his free hand on her face. When her eyebrows twitched, he took off his glove and touched the cool of her skin with his warm fingers. This would turn out to be a mistake, but he couldn't seem to stop himself from hugging her. It had been too long since he'd received any kind of affection from anyone. Dog slobber didn't count.

Liberty roused. Tate shifted her so he could see her face and said, "Are you okay?"

She nodded, but couldn't quite hide the wince. "Headache, but that's all."

"Aside from the fact that you're exhausted." She always downplayed it when she was hurting. "Can you hang on some more? It's not much farther."

She looked up at him as though he'd paid her the nicest of compliments. Tate had seriously missed that look in the last year but didn't want to dwell too much on the fact that he was soaking it up now. It wasn't going to help him when she left if all he could do was remember what she looked like. What she felt like. How she smelled. He had to get this woman out of his head if he was going to survive alone for the rest of his life.

Liberty straightened. "I'm good."

"Okay then." Tate turned back around to face forward and set off again.

For the first time since she'd shown up at his house, Liberty had seen the man she'd fallen in love with. She hugged his middle again, and felt the prick of tears in her eyes. Everything good they'd ever had between them... she'd ruined it all when she gave him back his ring and said she'd realized it wasn't going to work.

Which was true. Considering what she'd learned, there was no way a relationship between them would've worked. There was just so much unsaid now. She'd seen the question in his eyes, the pain of their relationship being torn apart when there was nothing either of them could do about it.

And nothing had changed since.

They'd both found some semblance of peace. Liberty could hardly believe that their lives now were what God had wanted for them, but what else were they supposed to have done? This was what God had given them, and it simply didn't work for them to share their lives.

Liberty wanted to ask Tate if he'd moved on, if he'd found someone to care about, but she couldn't voice the words out in the cold, dark night, silent except for the rumble of the snowmobile's engine. She hoped he'd found someone else.

Because she never could.

Tate revved the engine. Liberty saw something out of the corner of her eye and glanced over. Her whole body solidified as she spotted a man dressed in dark clothes, a weapon pointed at them.

"Gun!"

Tate shot forward even faster as the man opened fire. They both ducked and the shots rang out, each one as loud as a firework.

Blast after blast flashed in the dark, illuminating his position. His aim chased the snowmobile's path as Tate flew across the terrain. Liberty pulled her own gun out and fired back two shots, but the ride was too bumpy. She would never be able to hit him. Still, she gripped Tate tighter with her other arm and both knees and tried not to fall off.

Unless…

The shots continued. Liberty shifted back and launched herself off the snowmobile. She landed on her back in a berm of snow and heard Tate yell. He gunned the snowmobile, then turned it in a wide arc, coming back for her.

Liberty ran for the nearest tree so that at least there'd be some cover from the shots. While Tate raced back to her, she returned fire at the man who now sent bullets at both her and Tate in turn. Then he swung his arm back and fired at her.

Liberty ducked and the bullet took out a chunk of bark. She raced for the next tree, moving closer to the man.

The roar of the snowmobile engine raced up behind her. She glanced over, but Tate wasn't coming for her. He drove the snowmobile past her, toward the man trying to kill them. What was he doing? His weapon was in the backpack on her back.

Liberty shifted for a better position and fired to give him the cover he needed. Over and over. One shot managed to clip the gunman in the shoulder, and then Tate was in her line of fire and right on top of the man. He launched himself from the snowmobile and tackled the guy to the snow.

The vehicle they'd been riding continued on, but the engine lost power fast and careened into a tree.

Liberty raced over while they fought. The gun went off. She ducked and went to one knee. Tate had the man on the ground. He shifted, put his knee on the guy's elbow and grabbed the weapon.

Liberty relaxed one tiny notch.

Gun at the ready, she made her way to them. "You good?"

Tate didn't look at her. The man on the ground was bleeding, but Tate hauled him to his feet. Liberty pulled out her phone.

"Won't get any signal out here."

"So what do we do with him then?"

Tate shifted the man's collar. "Same tattoo. Russian as well, I'm guessing. Maybe the first guy from my house. He's wearing the right clothes."

The words weren't directed at her, but the man didn't answer. Didn't say anything. His face was deadpan, with no expression. No movement whatsoever.

"Guess we're walking back to town," Tate said. "We can turn him over to the sheriff, and Dane can get some answers."

That got a reaction.

Liberty saw the slightest movement. "Tate—"

But the man was already in motion. He launched himself at Tate.

Liberty hardly had time to react, but she was a Secret Service agent.

A shot went off.

Liberty fired as well, her aim true, and the bullet hit the gunman square in the chest. Tate fell back and the man landed on top of him. He rolled the man so their attacker lay in the snow. Two choppy breaths later, he was dead.

"Lib."

She stepped back, even though he hadn't moved.

Tate got to his feet. He stepped toward her, and she held out a hand, palm up. "We're okay, Lib."

She shook her head. "The snowmobile is trashed and we're in the middle of nowhere."

"We don't have to walk back to town now. The mine isn't far from here. Come on," he coaxed. "It isn't far, Lib."

"Don't call me that." She lifted her gaze and looked him square in the face. "Don't ever call me that."

They weren't a team. They would never be a team again, as good as it felt working together. Protecting each other. Taking down their assailant. Liberty had to let go of all her memories with him. Again. As much as it hurt, she had to walk away from Tate and let him live his life. Because one of them should have a future.

And it wasn't going to be her.

# FOUR

Tate wanted to hold her hand. He also wanted to yell at her and get her to tell him why she'd jumped off the snowmobile. He'd nearly had a heart attack when he realized what she'd done. Yes, she was a Secret Service agent. He'd been one as well, and that stuff didn't just disappear. He was wired to protect, and that meant Liberty along with everyone else. Feelings didn't matter. Even after she'd torn his life apart. Maybe especially. They didn't get to pick and choose who they protected.

*Thank You for keeping us safe.* God had protected them. That man had tried to kill them, and in the end had chosen to end his life by forcing her hand. He'd known what it meant to attack Tate one last time. It couldn't have ended another way.

Now there was a dead man in the woods. Liberty had taken a million pictures of the body while he checked for ID and found nothing, then noted as many details as he could in a text to the sheriff that would send just as soon as he got a signal. Liberty had said she would email the photos to Dane later after she downloaded them to her laptop.

Aside from that, there wasn't much they could do

about a dead body in the woods. Tate needed to find the plane so he could prove to the Secret Service—and anyone else—that he hadn't been involved in its disappearance.

Then there were the two men at his house. One had tried to kill him, and the other had planted evidence by leaving the plane's black box by his front door. The first had come back and tried again. It couldn't be a coincidence; there was no such thing in their line of work, he had learned. So it wasn't just the Secret Service pointing a finger at him. Someone else wanted to make sure he was implicated in this. But who? And what did they have to gain, getting him arrested and thrown in prison?

Liberty was silent beside him, and Tate didn't try to draw her out of it. He had no idea what was going on in her head, but when she was ready to talk to him she would. That had always been their way. What would be the point of making her talk?

Even though it had been more than a year since he'd seen her, a lot of who they had been together still seemed to fit. Despite that, he couldn't imagine them working as a couple after everything. But then, Tate couldn't imagine it working with *anyone* now. Clearly he wasn't the kind of guy any woman kept around.

Soon enough they were at the old mine, the place Tate had thought of immediately when she'd mentioned a missing plane in this area.

Assuming it hadn't crashed and there wasn't debris splayed across the terrain somewhere around here just waiting to be found.

If this was indeed a case of foul play, the plane had to have landed somewhere close to here. After all, the black box had been removed and was intact. It hadn't been destroyed or crashed with the plane and buried in the debris.

If the people who were doing this truly wanted the plane to remain undiscovered, it meant they had to be hiding it somewhere. The front part of this system of caves and tunnels making up the entirety of the mine was an opening big enough to taxi a plane into. It would not be completely closed in, but it would at least hide the aircraft for a while.

Tate couldn't think of a better place to put it.

Liberty stopped and looked across the clearing, at least eight acres of snowfall. "This is it?"

"It's where I would hide a plane." When she shot him a look, Tate added, "*If* I was the one who was behind this. Which I am not, and you know that. Or at least you should."

Maybe she'd never had total faith in him, and their relationship had been shakier than he'd known. But he'd thought they were good. Preparing for the future, making plans together for when they were no longer Secret Service agents. They'd been busy all the time, out on the road campaigning every few years. On overseas details, protecting the secretary of state and other dignitaries.

They had lived in some amazing places and seen some amazing things, but the strain of that life weighed a person down until they felt old beyond their years. He knew he felt it, but Liberty didn't look it. Her mom didn't look her age either, so he figured it was probably inherited.

"How are your parents?" Tate set off toward the mine.

Liberty strode through the snow beside him. "They're good. My dad won a golf tournament last weekend, beat all of his friends and everything. He was seriously proud.

They even got him a little trophy." She grinned, and her teeth flashed white in the moonlight. "Have you seen your brother at all?"

He'd told her the story about his parents' car crash when he was in college. It was the first time he remembered being really, truly angry. Tate's younger brother had been sixteen at the time and had spiraled on a downward descent since then. Braden had hit rock bottom so many times Tate had lost count.

"He doesn't return my calls. I invited him to Christmas, but I figure he'll probably just ignore the holidays." Tate paused, unsure whether or not to add this next part. In the end, he decided to brave the potential heartbreak. "The house I'm living in right now is actually our family's vacation cabin. I fixed it up so I could live there."

"But you told me it's for sale."

"I tried. I really did. I just can't face it by myself, Lib. I can't live with all those happy family memories and be by myself."

Liberty stared at him with some kind of wonder he didn't understand. "Tate, why haven't you found someone?" Her voice was full of so much pain it almost hurt to hear it. Like she couldn't believe he didn't meet eligible women every day.

It wasn't like they just showed up on his mountain.

She cleared her throat, and he let her change the subject. "Your Christmas tree is very nice. And the place looks great." She spoke tentatively, like she wasn't sure how the words would be received. "I haven't even had time to get mine up yet. And I was planning on going down to Florida anyway, but that isn't going to happen now."

"I'm sorry this has ruined your Christmas plans."

"I might still be able to get them back on track. I have a few days of travel left before Christmas Eve. If this gets wrapped up before then, I'll probably still try to head down to see my parents if I can." Liberty tucked some hair behind her ear, the way she did when she was avoiding something.

Tate figured she didn't want him to know her Christmas wouldn't be anything special, just a visit with her parents. It would be more than what he was looking forward to—assuming his house didn't sell in the next week.

A fire in his fireplace, hot coffee and a book. Sounded about perfect, but it wasn't anywhere near as enjoyable as the years they'd meet up on Christmas Eve at one of their homes and watch an old movie together. It had been a tradition, a part of their life together. One he'd dearly missed last Christmas Eve.

Right now wasn't the time to dwell on memories. Not when they had a plane to find.

"I'm sure that'll be great," he said.

She shot him a funny look, but he didn't have time to figure out what it was about. Tate led Liberty over to the mine's entrance. Once one of the most prominent sources of coal in this entire area, the cave had an opening big enough to accommodate heavy equipment. It stretched above their heads and to their left and right. The inside was a dark cavern he could barely see into. Good thing he'd brought a flashlight.

When they were close enough for her to see just how big it was, Liberty gasped. "You could totally hide a small aircraft in there."

"Me, specifically?"

"You know what I mean, Tate. This place is big enough

to hide a business jet like the one that disappeared. I really hope we find it and the people who are missing. I can't imagine what they're going through." She started to walk fast.

Fifteen feet from the mine's opening, a rumble shook the ground. Before Tate could register the fact that it was an earthquake, an orange fireball split the space between the roof of the mine and the walls.

The force of the explosion pushed them back onto the snow with a rush of hot air and flames.

Dirt and rocks rained down over the entrance like a tsunami of earth as the mine exploded in on itself. Tate grabbed her arm, but Liberty was already climbing to her feet and running. The roar was almost as loud as the deafening explosion. Her ears rang, and she thought he might be yelling instructions to her, but she couldn't hear. Thankfully, the terrain wasn't sloped, or there quite likely would have been an avalanche.

The ground started to shift under her as she ran. Liberty stumbled, and Tate scooped her up like the hero he'd been to her for years. Underneath he was still the same protective guy she'd loved. Being in his arms had been the safest place, second only to right at his back during a fire fight. And she knew which she preferred.

Tate picked up the pace, forcing her to keep up. Liberty ran until sweat chilled on her temple and ran down her back. She estimated it was almost half a mile before they were clear of the explosion and the debris it had caused, and Tate slowed.

Liberty set her hands on her knees and bent forward, sucking in breaths.

Tate set his hand on her back. When she looked up he

was scanning the area. Then he looked at her. "I think we're clear."

Liberty straightened. "What do you want to do now?" She could barely think. They'd nearly died. Her head spun, and it was entirely possible she was going to fall over. Just swoon and pass out, like she wasn't a Secret Service agent.

She sucked in a breath and squared her shoulders. Then gasped. The mine was *gone.* The mountain had caved in on itself like an empty burlap sack. Tate stepped toward it, but she waylaid him with a hand on his arm. "We'll be careful," he said.

"You want to go over there?" Was it even safe to walk over the debris?

"We need to see if the plane was in the mine. We might be able to get a look."

"We should tell the Secret Service." Not to mention the FBI and the sheriff. "There's no way that explosion was missed, even if it is the middle of the night."

"It's only one in the morning."

She glanced at him. He'd always been Mr. Night Owl, while she was an early riser. Something about the dark had always creeped her out. She didn't like being outside in the middle of nowhere at night. But even though she wasn't alone, she still couldn't relax too much. He would protect her, and she would hold up her end, but it wouldn't last.

Liberty looked at her phone, just so she could do something unrelated to Tate. His presence had always filled a room. When he was calm, that calmness seemed to permeate the air. When he was agitated, like he was now, she had to let him work through it. He'd told her he had tools he used to process his emotions. Methods for reining it in while he thought through what needed to be worked out.

She couldn't imagine it had been easy to lose his parents so young and suddenly have to take care of his brother full-time. He'd said it was going into the military that saved him and gave him the structure and discipline he'd so badly needed back then. He'd thrived, making it all the way to a senior NCO. The Secret Service had been a good move, though he'd brushed up against the bureaucracy more than once.

Tate was all about improving methodology instead of doing things the same way over and over. If it could be improved, it should be. Liberty agreed, though she was more of a follower than a leader. Some people were naturally take-charge people. She could do it if she had to, and she had in her personal life. But only when it was a necessity.

"No signal?"

She sighed. "Nothing."

"I figured as much. The whole mountain where my cabin is, I get nothing." He held up his own device—one of those ancient flip phones.

"I didn't even know they sold those anymore. Does it even connect to the internet?"

Tate shrugged. She knew he'd never enjoyed email and probably hadn't done a Google search in his life. The man still used a phone book to look up numbers. She'd called him a "dinosaur" about technology more than once.

Tate stepped over snow mingled with dirt and rocks, testing each step to make sure it would hold his weight. Liberty did the same, carving out her own path to his right. "The ground seems pretty stable."

"But the mine is toast."

She nodded. "We aren't going to be able to see inside."

"Still, the explosion might have made the plane visible. We at least have to look at it from all angles, in case we can see something."

"The FBI and the Secret Service are going to have to bring earth movers up here to clear it out if they really want to find out if the plane was here. *Is* here."

He pointed left, past the mouth of the mine that was no more. "There's a road on the other side. We can follow it out and get to town, get the word out that we think we know where the plane might be."

Liberty nodded. "That's a good idea. We can start convincing them you don't have anything to do with this."

"Is that why you came by yourself?"

She glanced at him.

"There has to be a reason you didn't come with your team. You drove out by yourself to my cabin." He paused. "I didn't think about it until now, since we've been busy fighting off guys. But now that I think about it, shouldn't you be working *with* the Secret Service instead of flying solo?"

"Locke knows where I am." Liberty figured it was time to admit the truth. "He wanted to wait out the snow, but I said I was leaving right away. So yeah, it was bad and I almost didn't make it. But I got to your cabin, and they should have been maybe an hour behind me. They were going to check into the hotel first." She shrugged. "I figured I could get a jump on proving you weren't part of it."

"So you *didn't* think I was guilty."

"Your mental state isn't the best, but it doesn't exactly scream 'domestic terrorist.'"

He gave her a dark look. "What exactly do you know about my mental state?"

"The blog—"

"Right, the blog." He lifted both hands, palms up. "I have no idea what blog you're talking about. I'm not even sure what one *is*."

She had thought it was weird that a technologically inept man such as Tate would suddenly start a blog. "About eight months ago you started posting monthly rants. At first they were just generally disgruntled, stuff about the government and how it's run. Federal agencies. Budgets."

"And you thought that was me?"

"It was all stuff we've talked about." What else was she supposed to have thought?

"I don't own a computer, Liberty. I have no internet access."

"I didn't know. It seemed like you, kind of."

"Kind of?"

Liberty shrugged. She'd hurt him, and when he had started the blog—or when the blog had started—it'd made sense to her he'd feel that way. She just hadn't figured he'd spew his feelings online. "What do you want me to say? I thought you were lashing out because I hurt you."

"And you came here to what…apologize?"

"Would that be so awful?" she asked. "I felt like I owed you something at least."

Tate didn't react. Not in his face, and not in his stiff body language. "The last thing I want to hear from you is that you're sorry. At least have the guts to stand by what you did. You tore us apart for whatever reason was in your head." He paused. "Does the reason still apply?"

Liberty nodded, unable to speak past the lump in her throat.

"Then there's nothing more to say about us."

Liberty nodded again. "It's good you think so. You'll be able to move on with no ties to us or anything else in your past." It hurt to say those words, but she wanted him to know he was free. He needed to believe she would be happy for him. "Is there anyone in town you're…interested in? Have you met someone?" Maybe he would answer now.

Tate's eyebrows drew together. "You *want* me to be with someone else?"

"I want you to be happy, Tate." It was why she'd let him go.

"Guess I'm just not wired for happily-ever-after."

Liberty blinked. "Of course you are. Why would you say that?"

"You made it pretty clear we weren't going to work, so why would it work with someone else?"

"Why would it not?" She hated that he thought this. She had to change his mind. "Of course you can be happy."

"And waste months—maybe even years—trying to find out? I'm done with relationships. Otherwise I'd have figured it out by now."

"Plenty of people find happiness in their thirties."

"Yeah? Like you?"

Liberty wanted to say something. Instead she just closed her mouth. What was there to say? Relationships were great, but she wanted more for Tate than she could give anyone, and a man who didn't realize the demands on Secret Service agents would never understand her life. It wouldn't work, and since Tate was gone from her life, she hadn't even been looking. She had thought he was her future, but that wasn't the path God had set before her.

A car engine revved.

Liberty spun around to see a truck round the corner over where Tate had pointed out the road. The vehicle rumbled fast over the ruts of debris, right toward them.

Tate set one hand on her stomach and moved her back so he was in front of her. Liberty glanced around the breadth of his shoulders. "It's coming right for us."

"Give me the backpack."

She did so, and they started to run. But before Tate could get it open gunshots exploded the dirt around them.

"Freeze!"

Liberty halted. Tate slammed into her, backpack first. He dropped it and slid his arms around her. She lifted her hands.

"Both of you, in the truck."

# FIVE

Liberty didn't ever want to move, and not because she would be shot by the men in this truck. Tate's arms were around her. Strong arms she had missed so much, it made her want to cry at the chance to feel them again after being alone for months. Just over a year.

"I said, in the truck." The man wore boots, jeans, a wool sweater and a leather jacket, and held a revolver on them. "That means now." Beyond where he stood at the open door, another man sat in the driver's seat.

Tate took his arms from around her and held his hands up. "No worries."

The man didn't look like he agreed. Tate put his hand on her back, and they moved slowly toward the truck. Liberty climbed in first, over the fast-food wrappers and the blanket strewn on the seat. It smelled bad. She glanced, once, at the backpack as Tate slid in beside her, and the gunman got in the front. The man turned, his gun still pointed at them.

He motioned with it to Liberty, and she saw Tate stiffen out of the corner of her eye.

The driver turned around. He was older, and also wore a leather jacket covered in patches. He had the same tattoo as the man in Tate's kitchen. They didn't have accents but were evidently affiliated with the Russians in some way. "Don't worry, you probably won't catch a disease from the truck."

Liberty had been attempting to ignore the state of it, especially the sticky thing under her shoe, but now it was impossible.

The gunman said, "Hands."

She lifted them, and the driver put a zip tie on her wrists, securing them together. He did the same with Tate, tying them so tight the strap cut off her blood circulation. Liberty glanced at Tate as the older man, the driver, turned the truck around. It was hard to stay upright, and she had to grab the seat back to keep from falling into Tate's lap.

She glanced at him again.

Still nothing. Tate's face was blank, but his gaze studied every inch of these men. The tattoos, the patches. All of it. She tried to see what he might be seeing, but couldn't. After a minute or so, she slid her coat pocket onto her lap and eased her phone out gently. If she suddenly got a signal it wouldn't be good. The phone would come alive with incoming messages, emails and missed calls. The beeping notifications would be a giveaway for sure.

No signal.

She turned her ringer to silent and slid the phone back into her pocket before the passenger with the gun saw her.

Kidnapped. What was Locke going to think?

Her boss *always* had an opinion, but first he'd have to realize what had happened to her. They might think she was part of this as well, and she would be implicated in the plane's disappearance. Liberty was a woman in a male-dominated profession. She was used to having to prove herself, and this would be no exception. Especially when it was not just her reputation on the line but Tate's as well.

No one else except her team cared where Liberty was, or what she was doing. No one would be calling to check up on her, and she hadn't told anyone but her neighbor—who fed her cat when she was gone—that she would be leaving.

The pang in the vicinity of her heart wasn't unexpected, but the strength of it was what hurt. And why? It shouldn't hurt when this was the way it was supposed to be. She should be used to it by now. This was the road God had called her to walk. But it was *hard*. She couldn't believe how hard it was turning out to be. Not that she'd thought being alone would be easy, but for it to hit her this intensely? Liberty blew out a breath.

The driver let his foot off the gas a split second at the stop sign, and then pulled out onto the highway.

The gunman turned back, and Liberty caught his gaze. She looked away, not wanting to have some kind of wordless communication with him. He would know he'd gotten to her. Yes, she was a trained Secret Service agent. But that didn't mean Liberty never got scared. The day she'd told Tate she was overwhelmed by it, years ago after a member of their team had been killed by an out-of-control truck, he'd told her fear was good. And how it was normal to be scared, but courage would show in what she did with the fear.

Liberty looked at him now. Tate still didn't look at her. Maybe he was scared, too. But he didn't look like he was. He almost looked as though he was…waiting for something.

She shifted on her seat and said, "Where are you guys taking us?"

Maybe these men were just looking for a lone stretch of highway where they could kill them and dump the bodies out of sight. But maybe not. It was worth trying to find out, if she could.

The gunman grinned, his teeth bright in the dark interior of the car. "Got a mess to fix."

"Are you going to kill us?"

"Maybe," he said. "Maybe not." The man tipped his head back and cackled his laughter. There was no other way to describe it. She'd always been the "good girl" and never acted out. Her parents had considered her wanting to be a Secret Service agent as doing exactly that. Like she should be a kindergarten teacher or a nurse instead.

Maybe they were right. Though, would a safer profession even help her? Liberty had never done anything really bad, even though she knew she was a sinner who'd been saved. No one was perfect, but what had doing the right thing gotten her? She had no life, no family. No real, true close friends. And not much faith anymore.

Nothing.

Tate had two problems. First was the gun pointed at Liberty, and the second was the fact that he was 90 percent sure the child locks on the back doors of the truck were engaged, because it's what he'd have done. Even if he subdued these two guys, they'd have to climb in the front seat to get out. Or roll down their windows and open the doors from the outside. Zip ties didn't count as a problem; Tate just had to decide whether to snap them before he went for the gun and waste a second in which the passenger could realize what he was doing, or wait until after they were out of the car.

*Mile marker sixteen.*

Rage burned in him at the idea that Liberty might get shot, but he continued to breathe through it. And count. His time would come, but getting angry only led to mistakes. Success was all about control. He'd learned that lesson by failing over and over again.

These guys were not professional kidnappers. They were, however, professional heavies. Whoever the Russians were being paid by—because guys like this never did anything that didn't come with a possible paycheck— wanted to get at Tate and Liberty. One or both of them. Did it matter? And whoever it was might not want them alive.

*Mile marker seventeen.*

"In a minute we should have enough signal to call in," the driver said.

Tate figured now was as good a time as any. Besides, the turn was coming up. The passenger who held the gun on them turned his head slightly. Big mistake. Tate silently thanked the Lord for the space to move in a crew-cab truck and launched himself forward. His bound hands went over the headrest and his stomach slammed into it just as he shoved the passenger forward, hard enough his head bounced off the dash. Out cold.

Before the driver could react, Tate grabbed the gun from the passenger and shot him in the thigh.

Liberty made a surprised sound, but Tate didn't have time to explain it to her. If she was going to object, she could keep it to herself until he was done.

While the man screamed, Tate yanked the wheel hard

to the right. The driver had let off the gas, but the truck hit the guardrail with enough force to bust through it and head down the ravine. This valley was shallow enough that they weren't going to tumble to a fiery death, but it was probably going to hurt.

Liberty gasped. "We're going to crash."

Tate held on to the steering wheel, his stomach still pressed against the passenger's headrest.

The driver, hands bloody from holding his leg, reached around. Before he could find a gun, or knife, or whatever, Tate did the only thing he had room to do. He elbowed the guy in the face. The man's head slumped to one side.

The truck bounced on a rock, headed for the river.

Tate yelled, "Hold on!"

"I am!" She sounded mad. Seriously? He was getting them un-kidnapped, and she couldn't be grateful? The woman had some serious problems. But he already knew that, so he just ignored her. Again.

The truck glanced off a tree, and the windshield splintered. Tate grabbed the gearshift and moved it to third to try to slow their momentum. Thankfully, it was enough; they didn't hit the water at full speed. Tate moved it down to first, and when they'd slowed enough he put it in Park.

In the middle of a rushing river.

He sat back. The truck shifted like it was going to start floating downstream. Liberty whimpered. He glanced around but couldn't see beyond what the headlights illuminated. Which wasn't much.

He lifted his hands above his head, then pulled them down over his raised knee. The momentum snapped the zip ties. It worked, but it also hurt. Getting out of tape or rope was way less painful.

Liberty did the same move, and her zip ties snapped as well. She hissed between her teeth and didn't look at him, just leaned forward and searched the driver's pockets. When she pulled out a phone, Tate commandeered it. She didn't say anything, but displeasure screamed from her shoulders and the angle of her mouth. No signal.

Tate used her phone again to take more pictures, this time of the two unconscious guys. "Come on. We can hike out and call the sheriff, have him pick these two up."

Like Dane was a trash collector, picking up the debris of Tate's life. He almost smiled, because it wasn't exactly wrong. It just wasn't what Tate had planned for his nice, quiet Montana life of dog training, taking shifts as a deputy sheriff and fixing up his house. Some extra construction work in those long days of summer, just to stay busy. Certainly not traipsing around in the snow in the middle of the night in December.

Liberty didn't move. Tate climbed over the passenger to get out the front door. Water rushed in at the gunman's feet. He jumped into the water, which was knee high, and winced. It was freezing. He waded around the truck and opened Liberty's door for her. "I can carry you, if you want. No point in both of us hiking with soaking wet feet."

Liberty didn't say anything. Tate touched her cheek so he could peer closer at her face in the dim light. "Did you get hurt?"

She shook her head.

"Then what is it?"

"You could have gotten shot. I can't believe you

started a fight in a truck cab and sent us careening off a cliff."

"It wasn't a cliff. The stretch past mile marker seventeen is a shallow valley." He paused. "I knew what I was doing, Lib." She had to know. He'd been in danger before, and she hadn't reacted like this.

"I couldn't even help."

She was a help just being there, but he couldn't tell her. There was way too much history between them for him to actually tell her he appreciated her presence. It wouldn't help either of them to say that stuff.

Tate turned, and Liberty held on for a piggyback ride out of the river. When he set her on her feet, he took her hand. Her eyes widened. "It's dark out. I don't want you to get lost."

Sure. That was the *only* reason he wanted to hold her hand.

Liberty wiggled her hand out of his as soon as they stepped onto the blacktop of the highway. She couldn't allow herself to get used to him being close to her. Not again. He was just being nice because they were in a crazy situation. Obviously there wasn't more to it. How could there be?

As soon as they had a phone signal, they called the sheriff. Dane drove out and picked them up. When he pulled into the driveway of a yellow house, he said, "Make coffee, and make breakfast. I'll go get those guys and be back in an hour."

Tate nodded and got out. Liberty said, "Thank you," because that was the way her mother had raised her, and then followed him inside. The house was cute, and the front walk had been shoveled. The snow was up to her elbows in a bank at the edge of where the lawn should be.

Tate was in the kitchen. Liberty found a bathroom, then entered the kitchen, where he was cracking eggs into a pan. Coffee was already dripping into the carafe.

Her stomach turned over. "I'm not really hungry."

"Me neither, but we need calories."

"We need sleep." She didn't want to argue about food because she was actually hungry, but it was after three in the morning and she was so tired she'd stopped having a filter. That was why she had to be so careful about not touching him; otherwise she would launch herself into his arms and start bawling about how they could never be together.

Instead, Liberty kept the kitchen island between them and sat on a bar stool. Tate loved to cook, and she'd missed watching him move around in a kitchen. Liberty glanced about and saw a picture of Dane with a woman in a navy uniform.

"Is the sheriff married?"

"Yup." Tate didn't turn from his pan. The smell of sausage made her stomach rumble. "She's the NCIS agent afloat on the USS Blue Ridge."

"Oh. Wow. So they're both cops then?"

Tate nodded.

"That's cool."

"Yeah, she's stationed out of Seattle, and he's the sheriff here. Long-distance, but they make it work. Dane actually said all the time apart makes them value the time they do spend together more. Instead of taking it for granted." Tate paused. "Some people know it's going to be hard, but they figure out how to make their relationship work." His tone had an edge to it.

Any comfort she'd felt over Dane's happy relationship—though she didn't know anything about it and was just assuming it was happy—now dissipated. Was she really going to rise to his bait? He was definitely baiting her. She knew Tate wanted answers. He'd had plenty of questions when she broke off their engagement, but Liberty couldn't think of how on earth to answer them. She couldn't just come out and say it, when she didn't even want to contemplate the truth herself.

Tate was just tired, as she was. It had probably come out inadvertently and she should just ignore it.

Still, Liberty couldn't help saying, "Some things you can't work past. Sometimes you have to let a relationship go because it's the best thing for everyone involved."

"So you live alone in DC, working all the time." He turned. "And I survive here, keeping busy and trying not to think about what should have been."

Liberty swallowed. He looked so hurt, and she'd done it to him. "This is the best way."

"You really believe that?"

"I have to." She tried to think of more to say, to explain it. "Because if I don't..."

Then all this pain would have been for nothing. Liberty had to believe this was best, or at least what God had asked of her. To let Tate go so he could live his life and have everything they should have had, just with someone else.

But Tate wasn't keeping up his end of the bargain he didn't know he'd made. He hadn't met anyone else yet, and he wasn't even trying! Tears pricked her eyes. One trailed down her cheek, and she swiped it away.

"Crying isn't going to garner you any sympathy, Lib."

"That isn't why I'm doing it," she said, reaching for a paper towel. "I'm just tired."

"When the sheriff gets back, maybe he can give you a ride somewhere. To your car. A hotel. Whatever." Like it was no big deal to him.

"Maybe I'll do that."

Tate shrugged, his back to her.

More tears fell, and she wiped those away, too. "Clearly you don't need me here, getting in your way. So I'll just go." She jumped off the stool. "I don't need to wait for the sheriff. I can walk." She didn't have her purse or keys and there was hardly a cell signal anywhere in this town, but she was resourceful. She'd figure it out. "I'll just leave you to your federal charges and prison time. Have a nice life, Tate."

Liberty strode to the door. Before she got there the sheriff walked back in. "Whoa. Where are you going?"

"I'm leaving."

Dane looked over her shoulder. His eyes flashed, some male communication she didn't much care to figure out. Then he looked at her. "The truck was still there, but those men were gone."

Tate's voice came from the kitchen. "They must have woken up and hiked out like we did."

Liberty winced. She was leaving, and that was all Tate had to say?

Dane looked down at her with soft eyes. "Stay for breakfast, Liberty. Stay so we can figure this out."

His wife probably loved when he spoke to her like that. It made Liberty want to do whatever he said just to see if she could make those eyes smile. Too bad she would never have the same kind of look to call her own, not ever in her life.

Liberty shut her eyes and ran her hands through her ratty hair. She probably looked like a total mess. Why wasn't it Tate asking her to stay? It could be, if she hadn't done what she had.

Dane said, "There's more to tell you."

# SIX

Tate stared at her back. Did he want her to leave? It had started to feel natural all over again, having her here with him. Facing danger together. He set the pan on the tile countertop, and even though his stomach rumbled with the idea of food, Tate didn't move to serve it into the bowls he'd set out.

Part of him wanted to yell at her to stay. To demand she give him…something, after she'd taken away everything he'd had. Okay, so she hadn't taken his job. It'd been a mutual agreement, and the best decision for everyone. Still, if he looked at the root cause, it was Liberty. And Tate wanted to know the answer to his most pressing question.

Why?

There had to be a reason she had broken it off with him. It had taken months to realize it, mostly because he'd been busy nursing his own hurt. Then he'd begun the process of going back over everything she'd said. Then everything *beneath* what she'd said. Because if Liberty didn't want to think about something, or talk about it, then she didn't. She just ignored the problem, even while she claimed she was "dealing with it." There hadn't been many ups or downs in their relationship. The first hurdle they'd had, it seemed like she had refused to face it. She'd just given up and told him to move on.

But if she was going to stay and face this, it had to be her choice.

"Okay, fine." She turned and walked back to the table.

Tate dished out the food like there wasn't a war going on in his head, trying to figure out whether or not he was glad she had stayed.

As they ate, the sheriff described what he'd found in the river. Dane blew out a breath. "I sure am glad you guys are okay."

Tate nodded.

"Just a couple of bruises, but I'm good," Liberty said.

Tate whipped his head around to where she sat across from him. "What bruises?" She was hurt and she hadn't told him?

Liberty frowned. "I'm fine. Like I said."

Dane continued, "Since there was no one there to arrest, I ran the plates on the truck first. Got a hit on a Vance Turin." He lifted his phone and showed them a picture.

Tate nodded. "That was the driver."

"Vance is the leader of a motorcycle club out of Great Falls. It's supposed to have close ties with the Russians."

"He has their tattoo," Tate said. "But what are they doing way out here? Does their territory stretch this far?"

Dane shook his head. "Not as far as I can see, though I'm going to call the police in Great Falls this morning and get the lowdown."

"Ask them if they know why Vance and his friends might be involved with a missing plane. After you ask him why he was over here, trying to kill me and planting the black box in my house."

Dane stared at him.

"I'm just saying."

"I'm going to chalk that up to you going through a stressful time and being sleep deprived, and not that you actually think I don't know what to ask fellow officers of the law."

Liberty got up, gathered up the bowls and silverware and strode to the kitchen with her back straight. Great, she was embarrassed for him.

Tate stared back at Dane and said, "Really?"

"I could ask you the same thing." Dane didn't back down. What he did was glance at Liberty, doing the dishes and giving them space. "That woman is dead on her feet. She needs rest."

Tate nodded. "We both do."

"I can see as much." Dane paused. "You can use my trailer. It'll be safe. I'll go get the dogs, let them out for a while and then bring them back here."

Tate studied his friend and couldn't help thinking there was something Dane hadn't told them yet. Some reason Tate needed to remain under the radar. There had to be.

"What are you going to do about…?" Dane's voice trailed off and he motioned to Liberty with a flick of one finger.

Tate shrugged.

"Are you willing to let her get dragged down with you if this gets worse? Are you willing to put her at risk?"

"She's already at risk. She's a Secret Service agent. We're both trained to handle ourselves. Liberty needs to stay with me, because the only way we're going to figure this out is together."

"Because you need her with you? Liberty could go, meet up with her federal agent friends. She'd be fine. She's here because of *you*. So make sure you don't want her here because of you, too. Otherwise she gets the raw end of the deal."

"She broke it off with *me*." Dane knew that. They'd had that conversation many times.

"Yes, but you let her."

"Is that even supposed to make sense?" Tate hissed.

"If it doesn't, then maybe you aren't the man I thought you were."

Tate felt the sting of those words. They cut deep from a man he respected, a man he happily worked for even though he didn't especially need the money. His cost of living was low, but the work as a deputy sheriff paid for dog treats and put gas in his truck in the winter.

He said, "Maybe I'm just me, and I mess up."

"Maybe you messed *this* up."

Tate didn't disagree. It had to have been something big for Liberty to break off their engagement instead of talking to him so they could work it out.

Dane pointed at Liberty again. "Best thing that ever happened to you. Isn't that what you told me?"

"That was a long time ago." Probably two or three years now.

"Never met anyone like her. Never felt like this."

"Dane."

His friend didn't quit. "It's what you said."

"She told me it was done."

"Goes both ways, brother. You gotta fight for what you want."

Tate had seen Dane do as much with his wife. In fact, he did it every day because their marriage was long-distance.

"But what do I know?" Dane shrugged. "I'm just a hick-town sheriff."

Liberty called out from the kitchen, "Is it safe to come back over?"

The sheriff grinned. They'd obviously been talking about her, but she hadn't heard any of it. They'd kept their voices low, and Liberty had let them have their talk. Maybe he was convincing Tate to turn himself in to the Secret Service so they could clear this all up. That would certainly make her position a little easier.

Soon enough the Secret Service would want to know why she wasn't at Tate's house anymore, but running all over the county with their prime suspect. She wasn't looking forward to having that conversation with Locke.

"Come and sit down," Tate said. "Maybe now Dane will tell us the rest of it."

Liberty glanced at the sheriff but directed her question at Tate. "Did you tell him about the mine?"

Tate nodded, and the sheriff said, "I already called in to the feds about the explosion, and how the mine is big enough to house the kind of plane that went missing. They're going to head out to the site at first light."

"And there haven't been any updates, no ransom calls?"

Tate turned to her. "You think this was a kidnapping?"

Liberty said, "I don't know. We have the black box, so that should tell us something—" of course, by "us" she meant the Secret Service "—and no one has found the wreckage. We would've heard more than that initial radio call if it had landed because there was an emergency. What explanations are left? Hijacking. An uneventful landing, maybe even miles from here so no one noticed." Liberty paused. "Like an abandoned ranch with an airstrip."

"Makes sense." Dane nodded. "There haven't been any updates from the feds in the last six hours, though the search is ongoing. They have the black box in their possession and they took the man from your house into custody."

"And the dead man near the mine?"

"It'll be processed by my guys and the information shared with the feds. That's how they want to play it."

Liberty nodded. "So they know someone is actively trying to implicate Tate in this."

The sheriff said, "Yes. The BOLO they have out for Tate has been updated. They don't just want a location—they want him apprehended for questioning." He paused, looked at them both in turn. "It's an upgrade from the first BOLO. They're taking a hard look at our man here." Dane pointed at Tate, who didn't even move.

Liberty would have been squirming in her chair if she were in his position. She couldn't believe Tate wasn't more worried about what might happen to him. He hardly seemed ruffled about any of this, even facing men who wanted to frame him. And kill him.

"You're in a sticky position," she said. "They know you work with Tate, and you're friends, right?"

Dane nodded.

"You're going to run into a conflict between that and doing your job." Like she wasn't also in a conflict? But that wasn't her point.

"We already passed the conflict-of-interest stage."

Tate chimed in. "So what are you going to do, Dane?"

The sheriff looked at him. "I'm going to be a professional who fights for my friend's reputation. I'm not going to let them smear your name through whatever mud they want. And I won't let you go down for a crime you didn't commit. So if you need a character witness, I'm it."

"The Secret Service probably figures they know all they need to."

"And the blog doesn't help," Liberty said. "It makes you look like a raging hothead."

"I didn't write any blog."

"Of course you didn't," Dane said. "You're a technological dinosaur."

Liberty snorted, and Dane grinned at her. He said, "I've already reminded them. And if they look into it, I'm sure they'll figure out it's just another way to frame you for this."

"Which means it was planned. And it probably looks like it *was* me."

Liberty glanced at Tate. He was onto something. "Go on."

Tate said, "If they had enough foresight to start the blog months ago just to make it look like I'm angry and wanting to lash out, maybe by kidnapping three people, then they've been planning to do this for at least a year."

She thought about it for a moment. "So it wasn't just the fact that the opportunity presented itself. Unless that's part of it. It could be a convergence of events making it all possible now." There was a clock running for her to check in with the Secret Service. What if it was also true for the person behind the missing plane?

"Either they were just ready, or something happened to make it now."

"But why Tate?" Dane asked.

Good question. "He came home—maybe that was the catalyst. There are probably a few who would have been good candidates. For some reason, they decided to pick him."

"A convergence of events?" Tate's expression held a touch of humor.

"Why is that funny?"

"Have you been reading snooty books again?"

"There's nothing wrong with the classics." Especially when they clearly expanded her vocabulary. "But that's not what we're talking about. We're discussing how to keep you *out of prison*."

"You're very cute when you're rallying to my defense."

Um…what? Liberty's mind blanked as she struggled to find words. Why was he being like this, and in front of Dane?

"Exactly." Tate glanced at the sheriff, a smile on his face. "Like I said. Cute."

Secret Service agents weren't cute. *Cute* was not part of the job description. And no one she worked with would have mistaken her for cute. Not the way she'd been the past year—closed off and professional. Liberty had pulled away from everyone, nursing her grief over Tate moving away. Finally admitting she'd done what she knew she had to.

Dane looked like he was about to burst out laughing. Tate figured that wasn't exactly uncalled for. He was acting weird, but he couldn't help it. What Dane said had stuck with him. All those conversations they'd had on the phone when Tate had been thinking about proposing to Liberty. Telling Dane all about how he felt about her, and how it was so different from what he'd expected. And even earlier, how Dane said he was in love with Liberty when Tate hadn't even realized it himself.

Tate watched her shake herself out of her flustered state. Even in the middle of all there was going on, Tate needed the lightness right now. Despite what she thought, he knew exactly the implications of what was happening. He could end up in prison.

His life was in danger, and so was Liberty's. If he let her go back to the Secret Service she could be leaving him with a target on her back. He didn't know for sure if she was in the Russians' crosshairs, but he wasn't willing to take the risk if she was.

The pleasure of watching her blush was short-lived. "We should head out." Tate got up. "You need sleep before you check in with the Secret Service."

"I really do." Liberty gave him a rueful smile. "I can hardly see straight I'm so tired."

"You should take my truck," Dane offered. "I'll tell the Secret Service you came here for help and I tried to bring you in for questioning, but you hit me over the head or something."

Tate wanted to laugh when there was nothing amusing about this situation. "I'm sorry we're putting you in this position. You could get in real trouble for helping us."

Dane shook his head. "I'm not sure what you're talking about. I found the flight recorder, and the intruder I arrested at your house, when I went to look for you. I've called and called you, but haven't been able to get through. The truck in the river was reported and I logged it, single truck, no occupants. Probably stolen. And when I did see you, it was because you turned up at my house in the middle of the night, took a bunch of my groceries and stole my truck keys, along with most of my weapons. After all those times we hunted together, you know the code to my gun safe."

Dane lifted both hands, the picture of innocence. "I can take care of myself, Tate. Don't worry about me."

Tate nodded. There was plenty for them to be worried about, and he cared about Dane's future—mostly because if he didn't, then when his wife returned from her detail she would box Tate's ears for it. She was gone more than she was here, but it wouldn't be much longer before she was home for good. Three years tops, he figured. At least that was what Dane had told him. They had a plan to start a family after she retired from NCIS.

Dane would be a great father. The thought of it made him wonder what his and Liberty's children would have looked like had they gotten married. Liberty was the kind of woman who would excel as a mother. It was hard for everyone, and parenting had its ups and downs, but she faced challenges with courage. He knew she would be able to do it.

Dane tossed him the keys to his truck. "Groceries are on the back seat."

"You knew we'd come."

Dane shrugged. "I figured it would be good to be prepared."

Tate wanted to hug his friend but stuck his hand out for a shake instead. Dane clapped his hand in Tate's and then shook his head. He pulled Tate in and they slapped each other's backs.

"Why does that always look like it hurts?"

He turned to see Liberty watching, her head cocked to the side. Tate wanted to hug her, too. She looked so tired she was about to fall over. He wasn't much more awake than she was, but the coffee he'd had would get them to the camp trailer.

Dane's phone rang. "Yeah, Stella." He paused. "Seriously?...No. Thank you." He hung up. "That was my night dispatcher. One of the neighbors called in a tip. Someone matching your description came in my house."

"In the middle of the night."

"Don't worry. I know which old-man neighbor it was—he never sleeps." Dane gritted his teeth. "Watches way too much television. They must have gotten your picture out on the news last night. Anyway, Stella had to pass it on. The feds are on their way here. Now."

Tate moved to the door and glanced back, once again regretting the fact that he had drawn a good man into his own personal drama.

"Go out the back way. The truck is on the side of the house." Dane waved Liberty along with him. She hung back in the kitchen, though. Dane motioned to a duffel, the one he used for the gym. "There are clothes in there. Liberty is about my wife's size. They should do."

Tate nodded, blown away by his friend's generosity.

"Do you want me to tell them I didn't see Liberty, or that you coerced her into going with you?"

Tate wasn't sure he liked either answer. "Say what you want." He glanced at the kitchen. "Lib, let's go."

"You should probably hit me." Dane braced. "Make it look good."

"One sec." She rifled through a drawer. Over Dane's shoulder, Tate saw Liberty tuck something behind her back. She stepped up to the sheriff. "I want to say thank you. For everything."

"You're welcome, Liberty." He turned back to Tate and made a "come here" motion with his fingers.

Did he really expect Tate to hit him?

Liberty swung her hand up to the sheriff's neck. There was a short crackle, and Dane crumpled to the floor.

"What was that?"

Liberty held it up. "Stun gun. Saw it in the drawer earlier when I was looking for a dishcloth." She hustled with him outside, around the house to the truck. "I figure when he wakes up, his story will be all the more plausible."

Tate started up the truck and peeled out of the driveway, praying the Secret Service weren't waiting at the end of the street to arrest them both.

# SEVEN

Liberty gripped the handle on the truck door, her phone now dark in the cup holder. She'd switched it off so she couldn't be tracked by any agency looking for Tate. She wanted to reach for Tate's hand as he drove, but he was concentrating. No headlights. Tate made his way through the neighborhood by moonlight. The clock on the dash said 04:30. Her eyes burned with fatigue. Liberty rubbed them and focused on the road ahead.

Tate hadn't missed a step. "Exhausted?"

"Sure," she said. "But also kind of wired. Though I figure as soon as my head hits the pillow, I'll be out."

Tate swung the wheel to the right. One tire hit the curb, and he pulled to a sharp stop. "Get down."

Liberty ducked. Over the sound of the truck's engine, she heard a vehicle pass. Then a second and third. If this was the Secret Service it wasn't her team, not with that many vehicles. This must be the other feds investigating the plane's disappearance. FBI, or maybe even local Secret Service agents.

When the noise died down, Liberty lifted her head. Tate's upper body was twisted so he could look out the back window.

"FBI?"

"And Secret Service, I think." He paused. "Dane's story should hold, but we need to ditch the truck soon or they'll use it to find us."

"What about you? You know you could just go talk to them, right?"

"And get arrested?"

"You don't know that's their plan." Liberty settled into her seat and re-buckled her belt. "The plan was to come and *talk* to you. There's no warrant out for your arrest, because Dane or I would have known. So you tell the Secret Service about those men who tried to kill us, and how they planted the black box in your house. Then about the ones who tried to kidnap us."

It had been a *long* day.

"I need more time, Lib. I need evidence the Russians are framing me and how they're involved. We need to know who's calling the shots and where the plane is."

"We won't know if it was in the mine until they dig far enough to see."

"Which will take time."

Liberty sighed. "And I'm supposed to just put my career and my life on hold until you're sure it's the right time?"

Tate gripped the wheel but didn't look at her. "Bet that feels kind of unfair. Like when you gave my ring back with zero explanation as to why our relationship—the marriage we had been planning—all of a sudden wasn't working for you."

"Tate—"

"Don't bother. I don't even think I wanna hear it. At least not right now." He paused. "I'd worked through a lot of it, and tried to make peace with it. You showing back up here all of a sudden is *not* helping."

Liberty didn't say anything. Hot tears pricked her eyes for the millionth time today. Why had she thought coming here was such a good idea? Telling him she was seriously, truly sorry wasn't a horrible idea. Truth was, the feelings she'd had for him were still there. Still strong.

Too bad Tate didn't want to do anything except remind her how badly she'd hurt him.

"Sorry."

Tate didn't say anything. He just let her single word linger in the air between them.

For coming?

For breaking up with him?

Tate had been everything to her. The perfect partner in work and life, or so she'd thought. Then came the moment that had changed everything. The moment she had realized she couldn't be everything to him. If they'd stayed together he wouldn't get everything he wanted in life. And so she'd let him go so he could find what she had with him…with someone else. Any other choice would only have been selfish.

Tate pulled out onto the street. "Let's just get to Dane's camp trailer. We can sleep, and then in the morning, when we're both no longer fall-down tired, we can run through everything we know and see what's next."

First thing in the morning was less than three hours from now. She needed to send her team leader, Director Locke, a message before she went to sleep. Tate might not want to make contact, but Liberty intended to tell her superior everything—including how she'd lost her sidearm in the mine explosion. She'd already lost Tate, and if she lost her job as well then she really would have nothing left.

Liberty stayed silent for the remainder of the ride. Eventually whoever was behind all of this would realize Liberty and Tate were alive and show up again to try to kill them.

Liberty shivered. Tate turned up the heat and moved the vent so it blew in her direction. But her feeling cold had nothing to do with the temperature. Even in the middle of winter.

Tate pulled up at a stoplight. The road was empty except for a semitruck coming in the other direction. A container on the back made the thing look like some great, hulking beast bearing down on them.

Liberty smiled at the imagery only a day like today could produce, and watched the semitruck approach the light on the other side of the street. It didn't slow down. Their light must be green. But instead of heading on down its lane, the truck veered toward them.

Liberty's smile dropped.

Tate said, "What—"

The truck still didn't slow.

Tate hit the gas, and the engine revved as they shot from the white line, the light still red. The truck came toward them, gaining speed. It started to turn.

"Tate."

"I know. There's nowhere to—"

Liberty gasped. They were going faster every second, but the semi was, too. Tate had them almost to the curb and the row of parked cars.

The semi hit their back quarter panel, just past the driver's-side door. Liberty gripped the dash and held on for dear life. The momentum sent them into the cars.

Metal scraped metal, and Liberty screamed. Tate roared, his knuckles white on the steering wheel.

Finally they cleared the back of the semitruck, and there was enough space for Tate to gun it between the car and the semi and get them away from the crazy truck driver.

Her breath came in gasps. "That wasn't just a coincidence, was it?"

Tate shook his head. "There's no way." He slammed his palm down on the steering wheel. "How did they know where we were and what vehicle we were driving? This is nuts!"

"Could Dane have—"

"There's *no way* the sheriff sold us out. He wouldn't do that. He's a friend."

"Okay," Liberty said, trying to placate him.

Tate shot her a dark look. Liberty said, "What?"

"Didn't happen to send any messages while we had a cell signal, did you?"

Her mouth dropped open. "You think that truck just tried to flatten us because of *me*?"

Tate just stared. "It's a logical assumption."

"And it can't be that it's yours?"

He shook his head. "My phone isn't even switched on. It isn't me."

Liberty bit down on her molars so hard it was a wonder she didn't crack anything. The man was completely infuriating, and she had half a mind to just demand he pull over so she could get out. Walk back to the hotel, wherever it was, through the snow still falling, and the freezing temperatures. "This is the worst day of my life."

Tate took a hard right. Liberty slammed against the door.

He said, "Sorry your visit has been such a bad experience."

* * *

Morning light streamed in the window and across Tate's face. He shifted on the couch of the camp trailer and stretched, even as he used those first few moments of wakefulness to thank God no one had found them here. They'd parked two miles away and left their cell phones turned off in the truck.

He lifted his watch from the table and sat up. Just past seven. If he slept any longer his schedule would be totally off, so he rubbed his eyes and got up. He glanced toward the bedroom area, four paces to the other side of the camp trailer. Liberty had slid the dividing door closed when she'd gone in there to sleep, but now it was halfway open.

Tate strode over and looked in. The blankets were rumpled, but their occupant was gone. He spun around, then strode to the door. Where on earth was Liberty? A flash of cold went through him. What if something had happened to her? He braced before he pulled the door open, wondering if gunmen were outside the trailer waiting to kill him. He grabbed the closest gun, checked it was ready and then flicked the tiny handle. He pushed the door open with his bare foot.

He'd forgotten shoes.

Liberty let out a squeal of surprise and looked up. In one hand was a drink tray holding two hot cups, and in the other was a white paper sack. "Tate. You're awake."

"And you were gone." He eyed the area around them, the wintry wind numbing his face while she entered, and then he shut the door. Liberty set the food down.

"You were asleep. And I was hungry." She sighed. "That was nowhere near enough sleep. But I woke up, and you were still sleeping. So I went out. I've been gone half an hour."

"Side trip to the truck?"

"I spoke to Locke, if that's what you want to know."

She'd gone to the truck? Tate couldn't believe she would do that without him. It was so dangerous. His stomach knotted. "And if there had been men waiting for you?" She would have been hurt, maybe even killed, and he would never have known.

She tore the paper bag open and grabbed a breakfast sandwich. "I am capable of being careful and keeping myself safe, thank you very much."

"I know you are." Tate knew there wasn't any answer to satisfy her. They would only get in an argument. The truth was, despite the fact that he knew she was a very capable agent, part of Tate went cold with fear at the idea of her being in danger. Liberty should be safe at all times, just for his peace of mind. Sure, it wasn't the reality of her life or the job she did. But tell that to Tate's heart.

He got a sandwich of his own and slumped down onto the couch. She'd been right about one thing—that wasn't nearly enough sleep. But they were going to have to suck it up because the longer they stayed here, the more danger they were in. Gunmen. Russians. Feds. It didn't matter who found them; it would be complicated no matter what.

Once there was some food in his stomach, Tate said, "Are you going to tell me if you learned anything?"

Liberty's mouth curled up on one side. She swiped her lips with a napkin and it disappeared. "There were a…few emails."

"Which means you had fifty."

"Fifteen voice mails, twentysomething texts and, yes, a whole lot of emails."

Tate winced. "Exactly how mad is Locke?"

Liberty scrunched up her nose in a move he absorbed like a starving man at a buffet. Apparently he'd missed that look. She said, "He wasn't exactly surprised I stuck with you."

"Oh, yeah?"

Liberty sighed. "I'd been at the truck all of a minute before he showed up."

Tate gasped, and a crumb of sandwich went down the wrong way. He coughed. "Locke *what*?"

"It's fine. He had the GPS on my phone activated. Apparently he's been tracking us every time the signal sent them a ping, and he was close by this morning when I turned my cell on." She sighed. "He's going to talk to Dane, get all that sorted out."

"He didn't try to convince you to bring me in?" Tate went to the window over the tiny sink and parted the blinds. "He's waiting outside right now, isn't he?"

"You think I'd turn you in?"

Tate shrugged. "It isn't so far a stretch from breaking up with me. I don't know what's going on in your head, Lib. And I need to be prepared."

"Sit down, Tate."

He leaned against the counter instead. "He could have followed you back here without your knowledge."

Liberty sighed. "Locke…cares what happens to you. He's here to convince the local Secret Service agents and the FBI agents who don't know you of the fact that you didn't do this. He's on your side, but you're so stubborn and determined to go it alone you're going to dig yourself into a corner Locke and I won't be able to get you out of."

"I'm not turning myself in."

Liberty gritted her teeth. He thought he heard a low noise from her throat, but couldn't be sure.

"I won't."

"Well, what are you going to do?"

"Find the source of all this." He sipped his coffee and thought through the plan as it came together in his head. "Find the person calling the shots."

"Easier said than done." She sighed. "And what are you going to do then? Beat it out of them? Maybe try a little coercion?" Liberty stared at him for a beat. "Is doing so going to help plead your case when the evidence stacked against you is so overwhelming?"

"Either you believe me and you're on my side, or you don't, Lib. You can't pick and choose." She'd stuck with him this far. If she left him and he had to do this alone… well, Tate wasn't so sure he'd be entirely okay with that.

She set her coffee down. "What's the plan?"

It took half an hour to get to the truck. Tate scanned the area for his old team as they approached the vehicle, but didn't see anyone.

"Locke is gone now."

But how far had he gone? The idea of the man waiting in the background, prepared to defend Tate, was baffling. Considering he hadn't exactly left the Secret Service in the best standing, he didn't figure he deserved loyalty of all things. Tate hadn't had anyone at his back for more than a year, and it had been a scary time, despite the fact that nothing necessarily bad had happened.

Now that Locke—and, yes, Liberty—occupied the spot, Tate felt safer than he had last night. In the heat of the moment it might not make much difference—if Locke was more than a second away and Tate's life was in the balance. But just the idea of them being prepared to fight on his side made him realize how much loyalty meant to him.

He glanced at Liberty and then started the engine. Maybe that was why her cutting him loose had hurt so much. It had been the ultimate move of disloyalty on her part.

Tate drove to the house Dane had mentioned the night before and pulled up a few doors down. "That house. The red one. It's the address the truck owned by our kidnappers is registered to." And the only thing Tate could think might yield any results.

"Our kidnappers?"

Tate nodded and pulled binoculars out of the bag. He seriously owed Dane. The man had thought of everything.

"You still remember snippets of information like that?"

It was just an address. "We broke up. Who I am hasn't changed, Lib." He studied the house—because otherwise he would get mad at her again—and then adjusted the focus so he could see inside the front window. Someone was asleep on the couch in the living room.

"Oh, no." Tate hadn't thought this could get worse, but apparently this day wasn't going to get any better. "Seriously?"

"What?" Liberty shifted on her seat. "What is it?"

Tate gritted his teeth, then handed her the binoculars. "My brother is in the house."

# EIGHT

"Why would your brother be in a place belonging to the Russians?" Liberty glanced from the house to Tate, then back to the house. It was run-down, even more than the other houses on this street. The front lawn was overgrown, and where some of the neighbors had empty driveways and mowed lawns, and others were just now leaving for work, the Russians' house had two beater vehicles in the driveway and a nineties sedan on the street out front.

"That is a real good question." He didn't sound happy, and why would he be? Braden was in there.

"Are you sure it's him?" Tate shot her a look, so she said, "It's a distance. How well can you see in there?"

"Well enough to know Braden is asleep on the couch."

"What do you want to do?" She wasn't exactly sure what his plan was, but she doubted it would involve sitting in the car and watching the house all day. Surveillance wasn't exactly Tate's strong suit. He much preferred action, and she didn't blame him.

Tate grabbed the door handle, but she waylaid him with a hand on his arm. "Tate…"

He looked at her.

Liberty hardly knew where to start, but decided to go with, "Be careful."

"I will."

"That's…not exactly what I mean." How was she supposed to put it? "I guess I mean it like, 'tread carefully.' Because what if your brother is there against his will?"

"I doubt it."

"But it's possible, right? Just like it's possible he isn't. He could be working with them." Something dawned on her. "Does he know computers?" Maybe Braden wasn't a technological dinosaur the way Tate was.

"Sure, I guess. Why?"

"I was just wondering if it was him who did the blog. He knows you better than anyone."

"I thought it was you who knew me better than anyone. How can Braden, when we hardly ever talk to each other?"

Liberty winced.

"We don't yet have plans to spend time together over Christmas, like most brothers do. Braden and I… It's complicated, okay? He blames me for a lot of things, like I'm at fault for everything wrong in his life. It's like he never grew out of that whiny kid stage where they knock over a priceless vase and then blame it on the dog."

Tate shrugged her hand off his arm. "I need to go over there and draw him out of the house. I need to look my brother in the eyes and ask him about this missing plane and these guys who keep showing up to take us out." He paused again. "Maybe it was even him who drove the semitruck right at us."

Liberty smoothed her hand on the leg of Dane's wife's pants. She'd thanked God the woman was a similar size, or she would be having a different set of problems right now. So far God had taken care of them. She could admit as much. They'd been in danger, and almost died several times, but He was protecting them. Watching over them. That wasn't in question.

If Braden really was part of this, there was no way God would allow him to be successful.

She hurt for Tate over the fact that he had to face the possibility of his brother not just disliking him but maybe also actively seeking to harm him. She didn't have any siblings, so she couldn't imagine what that kind of familial betrayal would be like, but she could see how it might hurt.

Liberty didn't pray for Tate about that, though. Because her hurt hadn't been healed. Not yet.

"You want me to tread carefully with a guy who might be trying to kill us?" Tate's eyebrows lifted. "Braden is a grown man who needs to take responsibility for his actions."

"If you go at him hard, he could shut down. Then we'll never get answers."

"Okay," he acquiesced. "I can see how you might be right. I can be gentle."

Liberty didn't want to react, but from his expression she figured she wasn't as good at hiding it as she wanted to be. She was exhausted, which never boded well for her ability to filter her thoughts and feelings from displaying themselves across her face.

"Okay," she said. "How do you want to do this?"

"You think I need your help?"

"Well, I'm not going to sit in the car."

"It's probably the safest place you can be."

It was her turn to shoot him a look, then she cracked her door. "I'll take the back. Make sure he doesn't get away if he decides to run. Or if there are others in the house. Call me if you need coverage for the front or someone to watch your back."

Liberty didn't wait for his response; she just got out and sneaked down the street to the house. The safety net of Locke knowing exactly where they were was a comfort. As was the fact that she heard Tate's door shut behind her, and then his footsteps. She wasn't alone anymore.

She crossed the grass and found the gate on the side of the house unlatched, then pushed it open carefully, praying it wouldn't squeak. And that none of the neighbors would notice two people sneaking around the house. Liberty hugged the siding past the overflowing trash cans and hoped no vicious dogs were hanging out in the backyard.

She stopped at the corner but saw only an overgrown lawn and no sign of animal occupants. Dogs would alert whoever was in the house to her presence, and she didn't want to take the time to calm them and fight off anyone else.

The patio was nothing but a slab of concrete with deep cracks and two ripped deck chairs. Liberty walked in a crouch to the window, then peeked inside. Two men—the same two who had taken them from the mine in their truck—faced a battered kitchen table, their backs to her. On the table was a laptop displaying a map of green terrain. One pointed to an area on the left side of the map, and from their body language it was clear whatever they were discussing was serious business.

Maybe even deadly.

His brother was alone, as far as Tate could see. He rapped on the window with his knuckles. Braden looked like he was still asleep, but at the slight noise he lifted his head and glanced toward where Tate stood outside. His eyes widened, an initial flash of surprise, which didn't spell anything good. Braden's gut reaction to seeing Tate was narrowed eyes and lips curled up in distaste. Like he didn't have time for this, even though he wasn't doing anything more pressing.

Tate motioned to the door, indicating to his brother that he should come out. Braden straightened out of the couch, his build very much like their dad's had been—long limbs, shoulders not nearly as wide as Tate's. It was hard to watch him move when he'd inherited their father's bearing.

Tate hadn't gotten much of anything, except his mother's ability to snap when she was mad. Her temper had been explosive, making her boys and husband band together in defense when that monster reared its head. Tate smiled at the memory of being fifteen, out in the garage with Braden and their father, lifting weights and waiting for Mom to cool off.

Braden opened the front door and lumbered out. "What do you want?"

It hurt to look at his face. So much of their father was in him, and yet Braden threw it away. Discarded all the good things he'd been given for the sake of solace found in substances that tore his body apart. Made his eyes red. Made his face worn and pale, looking older than he was.

"Crashed for the night with some Russians?" Tate asked.

"Wild party, what can I say? Sometimes you just fall asleep where you're at." Braden's attempt at humor was unconvincing.

"So you were partying with them. It wasn't just a ride home?"

Braden sniffed. "Why does this sound like an interrogation?"

"Maybe because two guys who live here kidnapped me and Liberty last night."

"Liberty's here?"

Tate ignored the comment. They'd only met once. "Those guys were likely going to kill us." He paused to make sure Braden's brain had caught up with what he was saying. "So I came here to find out who's behind a missing plane and the people on it, and who is trying to frame me for it all."

"Yeah, heard you were in some trouble."

"So you do know something."

"I know you're gonna want to watch your back." Despite his bravado, Braden frowned. "Didn't know Lib was involved."

He folded his arms. Braden didn't need to worry about Liberty. Tate would watch out for her. "Tell me what you know."

Braden leaned against the wall, a wry smile on his face. "Nobody tells me nothin'."

"You just said you heard I was in trouble," Tate said. "So where'd you hear it?"

"Around."

"How many people are in that house?"

"What's it to you?"

"Because they're trying to kill me. Or send me to prison." Tate's stomach knotted. "And Liberty is going to get caught in the cross fire." It was the only thing Braden seemed to care about.

The tactic seemed to work. Braden said, "I'm not getting involved. If you have a problem with the Russians, it's your deal."

"You won't even talk to them, find out who's calling the shots?" From the look on his face, Braden knew who was calling the shots. Tate pointed to the house. "You could find out why they're targeting me."

Braden didn't say anything. Which meant he probably knew exactly what was going on. Tate sighed. "Are *you* behind this? Because if you are, tell me where those missing people from the plane are."

Braden stayed silent.

"I'm not going to prison. I don't care if you do nothing to stop it. But I'm not going to let those people die."

"Like the way you let Mom and Dad die?"

Tate jerked his head back at the force of Braden's words. They were like a physical blow. "Mom and Dad's deaths had nothing to do with me. I wasn't there."

"I know. You were with me," Braden said. "I used to think you could do anything. School. Football. Girls. You were the man. Then Mom and Dad went away, and they never came back. You couldn't keep them here."

"It wasn't in my power to do that."

"Doesn't matter," Braden said. "I was a kid, and that's what it felt like. Sixteen years old, and you were my larger-than-life big brother who could solve any problem. Finish any fight. You could do it all. But you couldn't bring them back."

Tate squeezed the bridge of his nose. "I knew you were mad at me, but I didn't know this was why." He looked up. "Why didn't you tell me you felt this way? And why turn to drugs and the worst kinds of friends you could possibly find instead of talking to me?"

"My recreation habits are none of your business."

Okay, *that* was the brother Tate knew. Smart as a whip. Talk about being able to solve anything. The time Braden had fixed the toilet? Tate hadn't even known where to start.

"Besides," Braden said. "You left. Joined the army and found a life better than the one with me in it."

"I supported us. You were supposed to take the money and go to college."

Braden snorted.

"Instead you wasted it all on your *recreation habits*."

"My life is none of your business."

"It is now. You're hanging with people who want me dead or in federal prison. So which is it? Dead, or my reputation ruined and me incarcerated? Pinning a missing plane and three people gone squarely on my shoulders? Who would that benefit? Besides your ego, I mean."

Braden's lips thinned. "Wouldn't you like to know?"

"I'm pretty sure I already told you that's why I'm here."

Braden snorted out a burst of laughter. "I figure it serves you right, Mr. Super-Secret-Agent Tate Almers."

It wasn't the first time he'd realized his brother didn't just dislike him, but that he actually hated Tate. "Then I guess you'll have to go with me to talk to the sheriff." He reached for his brother, and Braden stepped back.

Tate followed him and caught hold of his arm. "You're not going to warn them I know. You're going to help me instead. Your brother." The two of them were family, whether Braden wanted to recognize it or not.

Braden swung around. Tate saw his brother's fist at the last second. He ducked his head to the side as it whistled past his ear. Tate threw a punch into his brother's diaphragm.

Braden's breath whooshed out and he wheezed.

Tate braced. "We don't need to fight."

His brother didn't quit. He swung again. Tate ducked and then pulled his brother's arm behind his back and slammed Braden into the siding. "Enough. We're *not* fighting, Bray." Their parents would be seriously disappointed with how the two of them had turned out.

Braden struggled against his hold. "I'm not telling your best pal, the sheriff, anything."

"I'm going to get to the bottom of this with or without you. But I won't let you tip anyone off to the fact that the Russians are behind this."

Braden grunted and renewed his struggle. Tate let go with one hand and pulled out his phone to tell Liberty what was happening. He'd just dialed the area code for Washington, DC, when a gun fired.

From the back of the house.

"Sounds like Liberty might need help."

Braden was right. Answering gunfire sounded. Two shots, then a third.

Tate was going to have to keep hold on his brother while he helped her. He pulled him from the wall but didn't see Braden's elbow until it hit his face. Tate stumbled back a step as pain reverberated through his head. His brother's footsteps fled away, and then the front door slammed.

Tate shook off the daze. He raced around the house and drew his gun out as he moved. Liberty turned the corner at the back, holding her left shoulder. Fear was raw on her face. "Go!"

Tate waited until she got to him, almost colliding with him.

"They're coming!"

She didn't slow. Tate glanced back as he raced after her. Two men rounded the corner. Tate found cover at the front corner of the house and fired two shots. They ducked down, and one hid behind a trash can.

The neighbors would call the police, and then surely the feds would come and investigate. Gunshots in a small town like this had to be part of the wider investigation, the search for Tate. What he wanted to know was who was out searching for the plane? The feds were completely distracted by all the evidence pointing at Tate.

He fired off two more shots, then raced after Liberty and caught up to her by the truck. Her face was pale. She pulled the door open with a wince. How badly was she hurt?

Tate turned the key and listened to it fire up. "You okay?"

"Through and through." That was all she said.

He gunned it out of the parking spot and spun the car around in a U-turn so he didn't have to drive past the house again. "Who were those guys?"

Liberty shook her head. She held her gun in her left hand, rested on her lap. That same shoulder was the injured one. Blood was visible between the fingers of her right hand, which gripped her left shoulder.

"That doesn't look good."

"Just get us out of here."

Tate glanced in his rearview mirror. "You'll have to hold on a little longer."

"Why?" She tried to turn to see behind them but

stopped and groaned. Liberty closed her eyes and rested her head back.

"Because they're in the sedan, coming after us."

# NINE

Liberty bit her lips together and tried to fight the pull of the pain attempting to send her consciousness spiraling into black. It wouldn't hurt anymore, but it also wouldn't help Tate. He'd have to carry her from the car.

Maybe after they got away from these people behind them.

"It was the two guys from the truck."

"Behind us?" Tate's voice was tight. He was concentrating.

Liberty didn't open her eyes. Her stomach churned, and she could feel warm wetness under her fingers. The bullet had hit the fleshy part of her shoulder, right above her collarbone. She couldn't lift her arm now, and the spot where she rested the heel of her palm on her collarbone did not feel good at all. Maybe it was broken from the impact.

But the exit wound under her fingertips boded well. It hurt like nothing she had ever felt. Still, in the grand scheme of things, it had knocked her down but not out.

"They were looking at a computer in the kitchen." He needed to know this information in case she passed out.

"Well, right now they're racing after us."

"It was a map. They were pointing at it." She took a measured breath while the pain threatened to make her sick. "Planning something."

"You heard them?"

"No. It was the impression I got from what they were doing."

Tate tapped the steering wheel. "Hang on." He turned left. Liberty could hear traffic sounds around them.

She opened her eyes and found they were in town. It wasn't like rush hour in a city, but it was busy. "Isn't it dangerous to lead them through this many people?"

Tate glanced at her. "More people means they can't open fire or they draw too much attention. Plus, we might be able to get lost in this crowd."

"But we need to know what they were looking at on that computer," she said.

"They're chasing us, Lib. They shot you." His mouth was a thin line, his lips pressed together. "We're going to have a hard time turning things around so we can ask them questions. It hasn't worked for us so far."

"Did you talk to your brother?"

"It was hardly a conversation." Tate held the steering wheel like a race car driver. "Braden still hates me, but we knew as much. He's likely involved in this and doesn't care I'm going to go to prison, but that isn't a surprise either. Go figure. The link between the plane and the Russians? It's *me*."

"And Braden," Liberty said. "Maybe by Braden's design."

She'd met Tate's brother once and he'd seemed kind of…sad. He'd reminded her of Tate a whole lot, even despite his problems and the fact that he didn't see them as problems at all. Braden seemed content with what his life was, instead of taking Tate's tactic of always seeking to make his life better. Two converse ways of dealing with the tragic deaths of their parents. She wanted to do something for Braden but didn't know him well enough to push him to seek help.

Tate's life had become something different since he'd left the Secret Service. Some of the drive he'd lost was probably her fault. Still, he was fixing up his cabin and working as a deputy sheriff. He'd retained the push in him to make things better—just not himself.

Was it because he didn't think he was worth it?

She knew how he'd felt about her caring for him. He'd told her over and over that her loving him made him feel worthy of good things when he hadn't thought he deserved them. When she'd left, had Tate decided that seeking out love for himself wasn't worth it any longer?

Liberty's heart wanted to break all over again just thinking about it. That was precisely the opposite of what she'd tried to do. Only *because* he was worth so much—more than she could ever give him—she'd cut him loose from being tied to her so he could find more.

With someone else.

Liberty sucked back a sob, and Tate reached over to squeeze her knee. "Hang on. We'll be out of this in a minute. I have an idea." He paused. "Can you walk?"

She nodded. It would hurt to move, like it hurt to think right now—or to think past the pain, at least—but she could do it.

"Okay. One more block."

"Are they right behind us?"

"Two cars between. They're playing it cool, but they've been tailing us since we left the house. Probably waiting for a quieter stretch of road so they can run us off and shoot us."

A shiver moved through Liberty's body, one she wasn't sure was entirely about having been shot.

"There's a coffee shop up here. Side door in an alley between two buildings. If I can get the car in there, we can get in the kitchen on the side of the coffee shop. The place has a front and a back door—it stretches the length of the building—and they won't know which way we went out. There won't be time for them to split up and find out."

"Good." She didn't like the idea of being on the run again. That was, if they'd actually quit being on the run this whole time. Safety was an illusion at this point, and she had the painful shoulder to prove it.

Tate made a sharp turn between two buildings and pulled in just past a Dumpster. Liberty's fingers slipped on the door handle. Her head swam, and Tate appeared in front of her. "Up and at 'em."

Liberty gritted her teeth. Tate walked with his arm around her waist, his shoulder right up against her good one. Anyone who saw them would know immediately she was shot and needed help, but maybe that was a good thing.

They moved through the coffee shop's kitchen, which smelled like cinnamon. The air was thick and hot and made her gasp for the cold air of outside.

Tate led her down behind the counter and out onto the coffee shop floor. The line at the counter was at least fifteen people long. Kids, families. Safety vests and name tags. Search-and-rescue workers and volunteers. They had to be taking a break from searching for the plane. Or they were all fueling up for a hard day of walking through the backwoods to look for the missing people and the crash site.

"Liberty?"

She knew that voice.

Tate didn't slow. He weaved through the crowd and headed for the back door. Liberty glanced over her shoulder. "Alana."

"Are you…" She frowned, then drew her weapon. "Tate Almers!" Her voice rang out and the room went quiet. "Secret Service. You need to stop."

Tate's body stiffened and he turned. He put his front to her back and his arm around her waist.

He backed up farther. People around them spread to give them a wide berth. Tate looked at her and said, "Just let us leave, whoever you are."

She wore a badge on her belt. The woman was Polynesian-looking, and her beauty was understated.

"She's the rookie who replaced you," Liberty said over her good shoulder. "Now Alana's in love with Director Locke. The two of them are besotted with each other and planning a wedding for next summer."

Alana's eyes softened a tiny bit. There it was. Her weakness.

Tate said, "I don't care who you are. We're not going with you." Not when he knew his brother was intimately involved with this. That explained the why—Braden hated him. But it wasn't the whole of what was going on, and Tate needed to find out what the rest was.

"You have a gunshot wound?" This Alana person waited for one of them to answer her question, then said, "Liberty needs a hospital, whether you like it or not." She stepped as he did, keeping the gap between them the same. At what point would she swoop forward and try to grab Liberty? To *save* her from him, probably. As if.

"Liberty will be fine," Tate said. "If you want to help, it isn't going to be by taking me in. It's going to be by figuring out who's ordering the Russians around. And finding the plane."

"You're going to tell me where the plane is."

"Would if I could, *Alana*." Tate lifted his own gun and maintained his hold on Liberty. She'd told him Locke was on their side. So why was his fiancée trying to arrest Tate now? Cold permeated him. Liberty must have lied about their meeting.

Tate said, "I've never seen the plane, and I have no idea where it is or where those missing people are. You tell Locke I said so. Tell him I already have Russians on my back, and if I'm going to figure this out I don't need his people there, too."

"No, you just need one of them at your front."

Her words made him tighten his grip on Liberty. She'd been hurt, and if she stayed with him it was going to happen again. Maybe even killed.

As much as Tate cared about her well-being, he couldn't forget the fact that Liberty was a Secret Service agent first, and whatever she meant to him came second. Her loyalties would become clear soon enough. Maybe they already had. And maybe it would mean the difference between prison and freedom, but Tate wasn't sure he cared either way. This time with her was better than any of the long, lonely days of the last year.

"Let us go." Liberty's voice was soft. "Alana, let us leave."

"Can't do that. Tate is to be brought in for questioning. This isn't about you, Liberty. It's about those missing people."

Tate said, "Blaming it on me isn't going to solve anything. It's just a distraction from where your resources should be focused—on finding those people."

Alana didn't exactly disagree, judging from her face, but he knew the push of following orders. It was Liberty who said, "Tell Locke we know Tate's brother is involved with the Russians." She stepped back, forcing Tate to move with her.

A few more steps and his back hit the door. He prayed there weren't any Russian gunmen outside, ready to shoot them. Though if they did die, Alana would do her job to bring justice, and those men wouldn't get away with it.

"They're planning something else," Liberty said. Tate's back pushed the bar on the door and disengaged the latch. "Tell Locke I'll be in touch."

She wasn't contacting him again if Tate had anything to say about it.

Alana said, "Liberty…"

Locke strode out from a hallway. Saw Alana, saw them. His eyes widened even as he pulled his gun. Tate shoved himself and Liberty out the door and took off running. He couldn't judge if Locke would pursue them or not. Tate didn't know the man well enough, not anymore. He'd been sure Locke would throw every regulation there was at Tate for getting angry and nearly starting a fight with him. Instead, he'd turned around and offered Tate an early retirement deal. He'd been flabbergasted, to say the least. What kind of person did that?

But he had no idea whether the director would help him now or not.

"Over here." Tate pulled her around the corner and glanced back. Sure enough, a bus was headed toward them. Tate gave Liberty his coat to cover her wound and thanked God for perfect timing as they hopped on board. After riding the bus farther north than they needed to go, Tate and Liberty backtracked and then rode another bus three miles east. It was a risk, considering anyone on the bus could recognize them or see Liberty's wound and try to get her help, but he just kept praying.

Faith was all that had held him together this past year. If it hadn't been for God, he probably would have spiraled much like Braden. He'd tried to talk to his brother about the Lord, but Braden hadn't wanted to hear about it. His brother was stubborn, kind of like Tate. And though he'd continually asked God why Liberty had done what she had, he still didn't have an answer. He was still waiting.

And now she was here. Because God had sent her, so he could finally understand? Or was it so Liberty could gain something she needed? Perhaps it was so they could find these missing people. He didn't figure it was so he could go to prison. God didn't allow bad things into people's lives for no reason. He allowed them so people would cling all the more tightly to Him, to persevere and have a faith growing in strength all the time.

When they finally arrived back at the trailer, Tate unlocked the door and made sure he scanned the area for anything amiss. He held his gun ready and had Liberty open the door with her good hand. When he'd checked every spot someone could hide in, he said, "It's clear."

Liberty climbed the stairs like she was going to fall over. He led her to a chair and found the first-aid kit, then cleaned her up as best he could using Dane's admittedly extensive first-aid kit.

He didn't want to say it, but he had to. "Maybe you should have gone with that agent."

"You wanted me to leave you by yourself?"

Tate shrugged.

If Liberty had any strength, she'd have hit him. Seriously? The man had wanted to ditch her at every turn so far. He'd been trying to pass her off to other people again and again.

"Sorry I'm such a burden to you that you're still forced to try to find ways to get rid of me," she said. "Maybe you should have just left me on the bus. Or at the coffee shop. Or at Dane's house. Maybe you should have let those Russians kill me. Then I wouldn't be bothering you so much."

Tears rolled down her face, but she didn't make any move to swipe them away. He needed to know she hurt as much as he did, and she wasn't just talking about her shoulder.

Tate touched the sides of her face. Liberty couldn't handle it, so she shut her eyes. His thumbs wiped her tears away as she struggled for breath. "I'm only crying because my shoulder hurts."

"I'll get you some painkillers." Tate didn't let go of her. "Open your eyes, Lib."

When she did, he swam before her in the blur of her tears. "What?" He was probably going to tell her the real plan now, the one where he ditched her. She didn't want to hear it, so she said, "I came here to help you. I came here because I didn't believe you could do what they thought you'd done. But I haven't helped. Things are worse than they were."

"Not because of you."

"You probably would've been totally fine without me."

"Yeah, it's been working so well the past year."

Liberty sniffed. "What do you mean?"

"Probably about as well as your life has been working without me."

She frowned. "What does that mean? We should be out looking for the plane, and finding out what the Russians are up to."

Tate leaned closer to her. "Tell me your life is better without me, Liberty."

She opened her mouth but couldn't say anything. There was nothing to say that wouldn't be a lie.

"That's what I thought."

"Tate—"

He touched his mouth to hers, and all the feelings between them rushed back in one giant wave. Liberty's head spun. She lifted her hands to his shoulders just to prove to herself this was really happening.

Pain tore through her and she broke from the kiss, crying out.

"I'm sorry." He moved away.

Why was he sorry? It'd been the best kiss of her life.

But all Liberty could do was hold her now-bandaged shoulder and try not to cry like a baby. *Too late.*

Tate knelt in front of her as she sobbed. He handed her painkillers from Dane's first-aid kit and a plastic cup of water, which she managed to choke down while she fell apart.

"I should let you rest. I'll come back later with some food after you've had a nap."

Liberty shook her head, even as she leaned back in the chair. "Don't go." She wanted to cling to him, though she had no right to do so anymore.

"What is it?" His face was close again.

"It feels like you won't come back if you leave. Like I'll never see you again."

"Not going to happen, Lib." Tate touched her face again, this time with just one hand. "I'm right here. I've always been right here."

Liberty shook her head. "I won't be. I have to go, so you can have your family."

"Braden hates me. I don't have a family, Lib. I only have you."

"We have to keep working this case." Otherwise she was going to say something she would regret. She tried to push out of the chair, but he didn't let her get far.

"Stay. I'll be back soon."

"Tate—"

"You need to trust me, Lib. Trust I'll come back."

She heard the door shut, and things got fuzzy. Before long he was touching her face again.

Liberty blinked. "Did you find them?"

"I don't know what you mean, but I found something." He didn't look happy. Not even when he handed her a mug of coffee and sat to sip his own. "Drink up. We need to move. The longer we stay here, the likelier it is that we'll be found."

Liberty nodded. The clock over the oven blinked noon, even though it was still morning. "How long were you gone?"

"Maybe half an hour. I went to Braden's apartment,

and I'm glad I did." He held up what looked like a checkbook. "He has access to personal accounts belonging to Mountain Freedom Credit Union's bank manager."

"Check fraud?" The fog receded. She could feel the wound in her shoulder, but not as bad as it had been.

"I want to go ask the man and find out." Tate checked his watch. "It's Saturday, so the bank closes earlier today—in half an hour. I'll make us sandwiches, and we can catch him before he leaves for the day."

Liberty nodded and rested her eyes for another minute before drinking two more cups of coffee Tate made her from a jar of instant coffee and a kettle on the tiny gas stove. The sandwich wasn't her favorite but she didn't complain.

"Okay, I'm good." She started to get up.

Tate waved her back to sitting. "Give it five more minutes."

Liberty nodded. She remembered Tate's reaction to her being shot. Touching her face. That kiss. She'd drifted off thinking about it, thinking how it was the best kiss they'd ever shared, and it had taken breaking up and being apart for a year for her to have that.

*What is going on, God?*

This was supposed to be for the best. Maybe God was testing her resolve, forcing her to be certain she'd made the right decision in giving him up. Or perhaps Tate was temptation—which wasn't completely untrue, since the man made her mouth water even with the mountain man beard—and she needed to flee.

Liberty didn't know what the right answer was. She'd been at odds with God for the last year, and it seemed weird to run back to Him now. All she knew was that in the heat of the moment she'd chosen Tate, not Alana and the Secret Service. Was this her answer?

Liberty didn't talk the entire drive to the credit union. She didn't even ask how he'd gotten Dane's truck back. How this trip would help find the plane, she didn't know, but she was willing to find out. When it was over, she was going to be the one to walk away. It was for the best.

"Want to wait here?"

Liberty shook her head and walked with Tate to the bank's front door. She wore a clean shirt that belonged to Dane's wife, which she'd been able to pull over her bandage and button up. Still, she didn't look good, and she wasn't fooling anyone. They were going to think Tate was mistreating her.

Inside, the bank was empty.

"Hello?" Tate called out. "Anyone here?"

Liberty turned in a circle. Lights on, front door unlocked. Someone should be behind the counter. Probably more than one person, actually.

"The sign is flipped to closed, which is weird."

She nodded but didn't look at him. Liberty walked to a row of offices and peered around a half wall.

"Hours on the door indicate they closed a while ago."

Liberty froze. "Uh, Tate?"

The nameplate said Gerald Turing, and she'd have been pleased to meet him even given the circumstances.

Too bad he was dead.

# TEN

Since no one started yelling at them for being in the bank after hours, Tate kept looking around. "What, Lib?" He couldn't believe he'd actually kissed Liberty. Apparently he'd checked his brain at the door of the camp trailer when he'd gone inside. But she'd been hurt, and she was so valiantly braving her way through the pain. When he'd realized she was a little loopy from it, Tate had left her to rest.

If the Secret Service or FBI had found her there, she'd have been able to answer their questions. Or simply tell them he'd coerced her into going with him to the mine. He'd have had "kidnapping of a federal agent" added to the list of charges they wanted to slap him with. It wouldn't have added but a few years onto his sentence if they were successful.

If Tate couldn't prove their entire assumption about his involvement was wrong.

And now he was almost sure Braden was involved. He couldn't prove much past the smarm on his brother's face, or the look in his eye, but Tate wouldn't put it past him. Ever since Braden had tried out for football and not made the team Tate had been the star of in high school, things had gone downhill. Their parents' deaths had only been part of it; he knew as much from what his brother had said. Braden had always looked up to him, but somewhere along the line, wanting to be like his big brother had twisted into this vengeance.

Braden's apartment hadn't been anything but a sad reminder of the life of an addict. Despite the fact that Tate had managed to find a checkbook from the bank manager's personal account, there hadn't been much else. No family photos, or reminders of their parents. Nothing more than a few DVDs, grimy furniture and a kitchen that desperately needed cleaning.

Tate sighed and continued his sweep of the main area of the bank, then behind the counter where the tellers sat. No one was here.

"Tate?"

He almost didn't look at her, as he knew exactly what he'd see. Pale face, tired eyes. Lines around her mouth to indicate how much pain she was in. He probably shouldn't have brought her here, but he just hadn't been able to bear the idea of doing this alone. As much as Liberty had hurt him, it was clear those feelings hadn't died. Would they ever? Maybe the two of them were tied together.

Still, it didn't change the fact that their relationship hadn't worked. Liberty had broken it off because Tate just wasn't the kind of man she'd been able to see herself with long-term. An answer he'd be given by any woman, not just her. Tate wasn't "future" material, or he'd be married with a family by now. And their lives were even less compatible these days. They lived in different parts of the country, which meant it would be even harder to have a relationship.

If he was even looking for one.

"Tate." She sounded aggravated now.

He spun around, lifted his arms. "What?" Liberty's gun hung loose in her good hand. She could probably still shoot straight. She'd always been an excellent shot. But he'd been doing a lousy job of protecting her. "What is it?"

"The bank manager." She stood by the open office door in the corner. "I found him."

Tate strode to her. "I can talk to him. You wait in the truck—you look like you're dead on your feet, Lib."

She looked like she was going to be sick. "Dead?" She also looked like she was going to slap him.

"You know what I mean." He touched her shoulders, not worrying about whether the bank manager could hear them. He needed to say this. "I don't want you to get hurt." Although that didn't make sense because she *was* hurt. "It's more than that," he continued. "All this is my problem, and it's sweet you came here." Now he knew she'd done it because she cared about what happened to him enough to brave his ire over her actions. He lived every day like his life was in ruins. Like the aftermath of a great explosion, leaving devastation in its wake.

Tate moved his hand from her shoulder to her neck, feeling the warmth of her skin beneath his fingertips. He *needed* to feel it, because Liberty was real. Maybe the only real thing in his life.

Which was why he had to do this.

Liberty's gaze searched his, her brow furrowed.

"You should go back to the Secret Service." When she started to argue, he said, "I don't want you in the line of fire anymore. Not when I know Braden doesn't care at all about what happens to me. This is serious business, and you should make sure you're good to go home and get back to your job. Your life is important and so is your job." He took a breath. "Because I care about you too much to let you stay here with me."

He moved closer to touch his mouth to hers in one last goodbye. It would probably be a source of pain later, but Tate didn't care. He needed the memory of her sweetness to accompany all the anguish.

Liberty's breath touched his lips. "The bank manager is dead."

Tate halted, his mouth almost on hers. He looked over her shoulder into the office. The bank manager—at least, he assumed the suited man in the chair was him—had a distinct wound under his chin. His hand hung down by his side and a pistol lay on the carpet, as though it had fallen there.

"Oh." His brain struggled to switch from what he'd been thinking about—Liberty—to the dead man. He moved her aside and stepped into the tiny office.

"Don't touch anything."

Tate turned back, one eyebrow raised. He hadn't forgotten that much. Deputy sheriffs of small Montana counties didn't investigate suspicious deaths often, but he'd done the training.

"They can't pin this on you as well if you haven't left any evidence you were ever in the room."

She had a good point. Tate stepped back. "How about you go in while I call Dane?"

Relief washed over her face. As she moved past him, Liberty touched his elbow. "Thank you for what you said, and for caring about me." She was quiet for a second, and he gave her the space to think through the pain to figure out what she wanted to say. "I'm not leaving you. I've come this far, and I'm not a quitter."

She went into the bank manager's office while Tate stared at the back of her head. She *had* quit. She'd quit on them when she gave up their relationship…and for what? Certainly not anything better for either of them.

Tate's words rang in her ears as she moved toward the dead man. Liberty understood why he'd told her it was okay to go, but at every turn so far it had seemed like he wanted to get rid of her and then brought her anyway. She was getting sick of his back-and-forth. Or she would be if it wasn't for the fact that he now seemed to want to kiss her to accompany his goodbye. Liberty would have rather had kisses that meant they were staying together, but she had to face the truth—this was all she would get.

Gerald Turing, branch manager of Mountain Freedom Credit Union, had been killed at close range. A gunshot from farther away wouldn't have left a burn mark on the skin under his chin. Classic suicide, shooting oneself in the head. Liberty didn't want to assume it wasn't murder since that was always a possibility until it was ruled out. Still, at face value, suicide seemed the most likely cause of death.

The man was older. He wore a nice suit, a string tie and a huge belt buckle with an elk on it. He was clearly no stranger to mashed potatoes and pancakes. His mustache looked to have been gelled, and his cowboy boots had been shined.

"Yeah, Dane," Tate said into his phone.

Liberty glanced at the man who had once been her partner in everything. He frowned, his gaze found hers and he mouthed, *They're listening.* How he knew from less than a minute of conversation was interesting. Was the Secret Service going to trace the call? It had been less than a day, but Liberty had expected them to descend en masse at any point, and yet they hadn't. Tate was their prime suspect. Why hadn't he been caught and brought in for questioning yet?

Tate paced the credit union lobby and explained to Dane how they'd found the bank manager dead in his office.

They wouldn't need to trace the call now. Liberty continued her observation of the body, wondering exactly how many minutes she had until the feds and sheriff's department showed up here with their guns drawn.

Likely not long at all.

The computer screen was dark. Liberty used her sleeve to wiggle the mouse, and the display woke up. Gerald's email was open, a message on-screen in huge letters. It was written in a weird font that looked like a fourth-grade girl's handwriting.

*The deal goes down. There is no backing out.*

"Tate?"

He moved the phone from his mouth. "Dane said they cleared debris from the mine explosion." He paused, as though he couldn't believe what he was about to say. "They found the plane but no people inside. The feds think I knew where it was and blew it up to slow down their search. They still think I'm behind it, and that I know where those people are."

Liberty couldn't believe they refused to see things from another angle. "We just have to keep working this to prove you aren't." She pointed at the computer. "The bank manager, however, was completely involved."

Liberty told him what the email said. "Wait, there's a

reply." She scrolled down and read it aloud. "'I can't do this anymore. I can't be part of this.' That's all he sent back, and the email address is about as generic as you can get. The feds should look into it even though I doubt they'll get anything back."

Tate relayed the information to Dane while Liberty thought it through. Could Gerald and whoever he was corresponding with about this "deal" be referring to the plane's disappearance? If so, where were the people who had been traveling on it? There was no sign of the senator or the two White House staffers. And what about the pilot? No one had even mentioned him.

Tate was being set up, but was this all that was going on? The plane and possibly the kidnapping of three people could be a simple case of a demand for ransom money, or way more than that. Perhaps all this business with the Russians, and the bank manager's problems, were nothing but a smoke screen hiding what was really going on.

She wandered to the doorway, and pain tore through her shoulder. She wanted to sit down, but she could hardly do that when it would contaminate the crime scene.

Tate took her elbow. "Hey," he said. "Come over here." He tugged her into the center of the lobby.

Liberty concentrated on her steps as Tate led her to a waiting area chair, and she leaned her head back with a wince. "It looks like suicide, but I wouldn't be surprised if the investigators say it was murder."

Tate's dark gaze bore down on her.

"What?"

He shook his head, but the intensity of it didn't lessen.

"If you're okay, we should leave. It won't be long before—"

Vehicle engines roared. Liberty looked out the glass front door where a stream of cars and SUVs pulled up outside the building. Red-and-blue lights flashed as men and women in bulletproof vests and waterproof jackets with ball caps with their agency lettered on the front jumped out, guns drawn.

Tate stepped toward her, covering her, but they didn't stop.

The feds poured through every door. A tall man with slick dark hair strode to the front as they were surrounded, at least a dozen guns trained on them.

Secret Service. FBI. State police. Even the DEA was here.

Liberty stood and moved close to Tate's back.

"Drop your guns!"

She hooked her lousy arm around his waist and rested it against his flat stomach. With her other hand, she held out her gun so the closest fed could take it. Tate hooked his arm under hers and took the weight off her injury. Liberty relaxed into him, thankful he was here and hopeful he could say the same about her. It just seemed right to move closer at a time like this, to close ranks, as it were, and stand together against what faced them. It was what she'd always wanted from their relationship, that mutual support.

The guy motioned to Tate. "And you." The Secret Service agent must be a local, because she'd never seen him before.

Where was Locke? They needed his support if they were going to get out of this without Tate getting life in federal prison.

Tate handed over his weapon. "Where's the sheriff?"

"Don't worry about your friend," the agent said. "Worry about what's going to happen to you."

An agent stepped forward and zip-tied Tate's hands. She winced when the weight transferred back to her shoulder. He glanced at her. "You need a sling for your arm."

All Liberty could think of was the last time they'd been tied up, and how easily Tate had gotten out of the same kind of bindings. He was making the choice to submit to them, and she respected him all the more for it. He could fight, though he wouldn't get far. He could refuse to help, but she knew he was garnering information that would help him.

When the agent grabbed her arm to tug her away from Tate, she cried out and clutched her shoulder with a hiss.

"Hey!" Tate moved toward her and guns were raised again.

The agent let go of Liberty, and she moved in front of Tate. "No one shoots him." She turned to Tate, her back to all those armed agents. "He didn't know I got shot."

"He hurt you."

She touched his bound hands with hers. "Sit down, Tate." Okay, so that wasn't what he'd thought she would say, given his reaction. He sat, but he didn't like it. A man like Tate, who was *all* man, wouldn't willingly take the lower seat when it was necessary to stand up for himself. But he did it because she asked.

Later, when there wasn't a crowd of people here, she would say what she had actually wanted to say to him.

"Good." She heard the agent step toward them. "I'm Agent Francis Bearn from the Bozeman office of the

Secret Service. We found the plane. Now you need to tell us where the two of you have hidden those people."

Liberty spun around. Agent Bearn had his phone raised. On-screen were three people.

Scared and tied up, but very much alive.

# ELEVEN

Tate was getting sick of explaining himself over and over again, but Liberty was currently being assessed by an EMT so he wasn't going to start complaining. Concessions would be nonexistent until he convinced these feds he wasn't the person behind this missing plane.

Nevertheless, he couldn't help saying, "Maybe you should be out trying to find them, instead of here harassing a guy who has *nothing to do with it*."

The fed didn't react, but Tate's attention was across the waiting area so it was possible he'd missed it. Liberty winced, but he didn't think it was over what he'd said. The EMT looked like he was poking her shoulder. The man said, "Looks like you'll need a stitch or two, and likely some antibiotics. There's all kinds of germs in a gunshot wound."

Liberty nodded.

When the agent, Francis Bearn—what kind of name was that, anyway?—started to tap his foot, Tate looked up. Francis stood over him, likely to reinforce the fact that he was in charge and had full control over what happened to Tate next. Which he probably did, but he didn't need to make a big deal out of it like he was. Tate knew the drill.

"Whether or not you had anything to do with the missing people remains to be seen." Francis tapped the screen on his phone. "It's been thirty-six hours since the plane went missing, and right now cooperation is the name of the game."

"I don't need to see the picture again. I don't know where they're being held, but it looks like an empty room to me. Not sure that's going to help find them."

"That's not what I intend to show you."

Tate figured the man's displeasure was due to the fact that he hadn't been on a presidential detail in at least a decade. He was old enough he'd probably been a Secret Service agent for at least that long, if not longer, but Tate had never met him. Francis could've been here in Montana, and slipped through the cracks of promotion, never making it to Washington.

Tate would probably be mad if it had happened to him. Whether or not he'd channel the feeling into making a suspect in a missing persons case feel like the worst criminal in the world, well—he'd like to say he'd be professional enough not to make this personal, but he'd never been accused of taking a back seat.

Tate had been written up a few times, but for nothing more than infractions. It had happened in the army as well, so he'd figured it was just his personality. Some people didn't like those who inserted themselves into a situation when something didn't sit right with them. And in the old-boy's network of the Secret Service, it had happened a few times. Agents like Liberty and the rookie female he'd met in the coffee shop, Alana, didn't deserve to be treated like they weren't as good as all the male agents just because they were women. They didn't deserve to get called "Little Darlin'" and asked to fetch coffee for the men. They were agents, just like the rest.

Francis turned the phone toward Tate. "This is the first video we received."

"Video?" He'd thought it was just a picture.

The screen came to life, dark images and the muffled sounds of someone blowing into a microphone. The image panned to the first person: a suited man, the senator from Oklahoma.

He swallowed. "My name is Edward Frampton."

The camera panned farther out, to a woman in a white blouse and dark-colored skirt. Her hair was falling out of whatever she'd fastened it up with, and her face was streaked with dirt and tears. Her voice was shaky when she said, "My name is Bethany Piers."

The last person was a man, younger and thinner than the senator. The other White House staffer, along with Bethany. He lifted his chin. "My name is Anthony Wills."

The camera shifted, turned all the way around to a man in a ski mask. "And my name is Tate Almers."

Tate felt his eyes widen. He tried to place the voice, but it was a little distorted, so it was difficult.

Francis hit pause. "This is the third video, and the one where he makes his demands."

The Tate wannabe said, "Now that we're all acquainted, I'll lay out what I want. Two million dollars in nonsequential bills. No hidden GPS trackers either. And the release of Puerto Alvarez. I'll help you out—he's at Atwater. I'll text the address for the drop. You have twenty-four hours."

Francis paused the video and said, "That gives us

until six tonight. Only a few hours from now. And the length of time means he knows it'll take a while to get Alvarez here."

"That wasn't me." Tate looked at the wall clock. It wasn't even two in the afternoon, and they'd received this video message hours before Liberty had even shown up at his house. Was that really just yesterday? It felt like a week.

Liberty pushed away the EMT and strode over, her face pinched. "Of course it wasn't Tate in the video! Any fool could hear a difference in the voices. It actually kind of sounded like—"

Tate shot her a look, then shook his head. The distortion had been there, but it wasn't enough to cover it completely. He knew what Liberty was thinking. After all, his brother's hatred of him had been their biggest topic of conversation today. But Tate couldn't be certain.

And why would Braden be demanding the release of an inmate from a prison in California? Atwater was a high-security federal prison.

Liberty snapped her head around to where Francis stood watching their interplay. Tate was innocent. Francis needed to believe it, and Tate figured he needed to at least trust Liberty as a fellow agent.

"Since when have we been receiving ransom demands, anyway?" she said. "That's the first I've heard about it. This should have been mentioned on the news, maybe, don't you think?" She glanced around, looking for someone to agree with her. "Or I don't know, maybe *to the Secret Service.*"

"If you're referring to Director James Locke," Francis said, "he knows."

"He..." Liberty broke off, stuttering.

"The director has been fully briefed."

Tate wanted to ask Liberty to sit down before she popped a blood vessel getting all worked up, but he didn't think it would go down well.

She said, "I can't believe this. I would have been told."

"Lib." Tate needed her to calm down.

She pressed her lips into a thin line, then glanced at the ceiling like she was praying for assistance. How was her relationship with God? They'd gone to church together when they were engaged, but she hadn't mentioned Him since she got here.

Tate could use some quiet time with his Bible, but he hadn't stopped praying this whole time. It seemed like things were only getting worse—for the investigation at least. Things between him and Liberty were actually pretty good considering they'd kissed, and right now she was poised and ready to defend him.

Tate nearly smiled, but instead he said, "How was that video sent?"

"It was broadcast live on a social media account. We've looked into it, and it's an anonymous profile as far as we could tell. It was set up minutes before the first broadcast and is still open, which means they aren't worried it will get traced. Which likely means they've covered their tracks. But we are looking into it."

Francis folded his arms. "There have been two more videos so far. The first one got some attention, but we managed to squash it with a virus before it spread. And before the media turned this whole thing into a circus." He looked pointedly at Liberty. "The next two we kept from public view. In each video, the kidnapper claims to be you." He pointed at Tate. "And in one we see a wider view of him."

"And?" It had to be significant for Francis to bring it up.

"You're more muscled than him. He was skinny."

Liberty glanced at him, her eyes sad. "Braden."

Tate shrugged. "If you didn't think it was me, why have you been hunting me this whole time?"

Francis didn't answer. He just said, "Do you think your brother could do something like this?"

Tate shrugged, his attention drawn to the huddle of DEA agents in the corner. All three of them had pulled out their phones and were now typing furiously.

If he was running this investigation and the search for these people, he'd be chasing down Tate as his most solid source of leads as well. It made sense. "I wouldn't put it past Braden to do something like this. Or at least he might *want* to. It's the effort he'd have to put into the execution that I'm having trouble believing." He told Francis about the conversation at the house.

"So he is involved."

"Maybe the map on the computer wasn't something that's going to happen," Liberty said. "What if it already has happened? What if it was where they're keeping the people they kidnapped?" She turned to Francis. "Were you able to get a location from the video?"

"Each of the three were recorded in a new location. By the time we get to it, even minutes after the broadcast is over, they're already gone."

"So they find a place with Wi-Fi, log in and make the video, and then move on?" When Francis nodded, Liberty said, "That's clever. And completely frustrating."

Tate nodded. "Yes, it is."

"I'll put the word out, have your brother found and brought in."

He nodded to Francis this time, but didn't say anything. What was there to say? Braden had engineered this whole thing, or at least the fact that it was being blamed on Tate. What kind of brother was he when his own flesh and blood wanted to do this to him? He really hated Tate that much?

"And in the meantime," Tate said, "we do what? Wait for another broadcast, chase them down and find nothing?" Assuming the feds weren't actually planning to hand a federal prisoner over to this kidnapper.

"We're investigating, but we're also prepping to make the transaction," Francis said. "It's our best shot at catching this guy and making him tell us where the people are."

Tate sighed. "We need more."

The alternative would be devastating to the families of the missing people.

Liberty wanted to pace. Or throw something. Or yell at someone. Instead she stopped and shut her eyes for a second, taking a moment to pray. She was just lifting her head when Locke walked in, closely followed by Alana. The two were never far apart, even if to an outsider it would appear they had only a close working relationship. They had set the bar on having a professional attitude about their romance. Liberty felt a pang of…shame, maybe, when she thought about how she and Tate had been.

Sneaking kisses when no one was looking had been fun and all, but was hardly professional even if no one had caught them. Love made people act crazy, though. Everyone said so. Still, if she could go back, she'd do it all differently.

But she would still do it all again. Because, as much as it hurt now, she'd needed him back then. She'd needed to feel…well, needed. Who didn't? Liberty couldn't even describe the feeling, knowing Tate loved her as much as he'd shown her he had.

"Lib?"

She glanced at Tate and shook her head. There was no reason to drag up the past, even if standing here made it feel like they could just slide right back into the place where they'd been so in love. The future had stretched out ahead of them, so far. So bright. Then with one diagnosis, the steel bars of a cell had slammed down over Liberty's life, and she'd realized she could never give Tate everything he wanted.

"Are you okay?" Alana's face was open. She'd probably never seen this version of Liberty. Since Tate's leaving she'd been closed off. Antisocial, and nursing her wounds. She'd pulled away from everyone.

Liberty didn't even know what to tell her. "Once we get this cleared up, I probably will be." She turned to Locke and said, "Want to tell me why you never mentioned videos when we talked?"

Locke shrugged. "I compartmentalized information in order to provide you with the best possible focus."

"Meaning you lied to me."

"Withholding information as your boss is not the same thing as lying, Agent Westmark." Locke wasn't going to apologize when he was convinced he'd done the right thing. Alana's brow held a tiny line, which Liberty figured meant she didn't completely agree, but Liberty wasn't going to mention it.

Her arm hurt enough that she'd like to just yell at all of them, when it wouldn't be completely warranted.

Why did she do that when she was in pain? She should probably ask Tate, since it was what he'd done when she had broken up with him. However, that might not be a tactful question.

Liberty slumped into a chair and leaned back gently until her back touched the wall.

"You okay?" Tate's question was low and quiet, for her ears only.

She turned her head and found his face close. "The EMT gave me a shot, and it's supposed to kick in soon." She shut her eyes. "I feel like we've been one step behind this entire time. Everyone seems to have more information about this than we do."

Tate shifted beside her. "Yes, it does feel that way." He paused. "Makes me wonder what else they haven't told us."

"You're not Secret Service," Francis said, with no apology in his tone.

Locke moved to stand beside the local agent. "And Liberty was compromised."

Her eyes flew open, but Tate waylaid her with a hand on her arm. She said, "Gee, thanks, boss." Okay, so he was telling the truth. Still, did she want him saying so in front of Tate and everyone else? Not especially.

Locke said, "Your emotions are all tied up in this, and don't bother denying it. So we kept a close eye on you. The sheriff filled in the rest."

They'd been watching this whole time? That was probably why nobody had stormed into the camp trailer and taken Tate into custody. Tate had probably figured it was the fact that she'd made contact with her boss, but it was evidently also because the feds had been on their tails whenever they had a cell signal.

"So why make contact now?" Tate's question was one she wanted to ask as well.

"Apart from the dead man over there?" Francis lifted one eyebrow but didn't look to where investigators processed every inch of the office while the medical examiner peered at the body. "We're running out of time until the deadline, and we need you to make contact with your brother."

"You think I can find him?"

"You've done it already. There's no reason to assume you can't again."

Tate's jaw flexed. Liberty wanted to help, but what was she supposed to do? She wasn't going to figure this out alone. Only by all of them working as a team would they find those missing people. All of them, including Tate.

"So you don't think Tate is involved?" she asked them all. "You think Tate's name is clear, and he can help by finding his brother?"

"I still want proof beyond a doubt he's not part of this," Francis said. "So far it's just circumstantial, but I figure it won't be totally confirmed until this is over and we take it all apart. At least for now, I'm satisfied." He pinned Tate with a stare. "As long as you stay close."

"You're keeping me on a short leash?" Tate didn't sound pleased about it.

Francis nodded. Tate said, "And Dane? You know he's not part of this either, right?"

"The sheriff is facing no charges at this time, and I suspect not in the future either."

Liberty figured that was probably the best they were going to get, considering Dane had technically become an accessory. Still, they weren't far past assuming Tate was guilty, which he wasn't. The whole thing was up in the air until they could prove for good who was actually behind the missing people.

She turned to Tate. "So we go find your brother?"

Tate shrugged. "I guess. We can backtrack, visit some of his haunts."

"We could go to his apartment together this time," Liberty said.

She knew Tate didn't miss her tone. He just chose to ignore it and said, "We can visit some of his friends as well."

"You'll want to start with the girlfriend," Francis said.

Tate's head jerked. "Braden has a girlfriend?"

Francis frowned. "Yes, the mother of your niece."

# TWELVE

"I cannot believe they didn't tell me about the videos."

Tate flicked on his blinker and glanced in the rearview at the government SUV behind them. No one had asked questions about the fact that they were still driving Dane's truck, which he'd told the feds they had stolen. That was the least of everyone's problems right now. Braden hadn't been at the house where Liberty got shot, and neither had the Russians. It had been entirely cleaned out.

Now they were headed to the address Francis had given them so the agent could listen to whatever conversation they might have with Braden's girlfriend. The one who was the mother of his child.

Tate could hardly wrap his head around it.

"Are you even listening to me?"

The feds had likely already activated the listening device, hoping they'd hear something incriminating. Everyone in the SUV behind them was probably busting up laughing at Liberty's "complaining wife" routine.

Tate glanced at her and kept driving. "Locke didn't think you were compromised because of your feelings. He knows you better than that, Lib."

"Does he?" She overexaggerated the question. "You don't know what he was thinking. Maybe I've gone off the deep end in the last year. Maybe I've been taking things too personally and he can't trust me to be a professional." She paused long enough to take in more air and start up again. "I've done nothing *but* be a professional this past year."

Part of Tate didn't want to know the answer to his next question, but also a part of him needed to know. "How have you been?"

Liberty's head flicked around in his direction, but he kept his eyes on the road instead of on her. She said, "How have I been?"

Tate shrugged.

"How do you think I've been?" she asked. "Lonely, Tate. I've been very, very lonely. But the frozen tundra of my personal life has nothing to do with my ability to do my job."

He wanted to explain how it was her fault, given he wouldn't have left if she hadn't broken their engagement. But was he going to mention it right now? No. "This might just be one of those things you've gotta let go, Lib. Locke made a decision and it's done. You don't like it, but there's nothing you can do. Can't go back in time and change the past."

He made a left turn and felt her hand touch his forearm. Her good hand, since she hugged the other arm to her body. The EMT had said she needed to see a doctor, get stitched up and get a prescription. And yet, she was here with him still.

He didn't know what it meant, and he also didn't know if he was okay with it. Tate wasn't a better option than delaying medical attention.

"Is that how you feel about what I did?"

Why were they even talking about this? He should be laying out the plan for how they were going to talk to his brother's girlfriend. The one who was the mother of his niece. At the very least, they should be talking about *that*. He hadn't had the first clue his brother had a child.

"Does it matter how I feel?" Tate shrugged his shoulder, but she kept hold of his arm. "It's done, right? Decision made. Thank you very much. Don't worry about how I'm gonna feel."

Liberty's hand slid from his arm then, and she swiped at her face. Great. Now he'd made her cry.

"Look, it doesn't matter." He didn't really know what else to say.

"It does matter." A sob hitched in her throat. He heard her try to hide it. "I'm sorry, Tate. I'm really sorry."

"We were together for two years, Lib, and engaged for six months. I thought I was going to spend the rest of my life with you, and then one day you just broke it off." He waited until he pulled up at a red light and then turned to her, uncaring whether or not anyone was listening. "Why, Lib? Why did you do it? And don't give me the same 'it's not going to work' reason. Because I don't believe it."

Liberty set her hand on her shoulder, over where she'd been hit by the bullet. Her body curved forward, her eyes squeezed and she jerked with each sob.

"Tell me why."

She shook her head without opening her eyes or looking at him. "I can't." Her voice was a whisper.

Tate stared at her.

Someone honked. The light was green. Tate pulled

away from the line and headed for the address Francis had given them.

What else was there to say? If Liberty wasn't going to tell him the real reason she'd broken their engagement, what was the point in pushing her?

While she collected herself, Tate found the house number. He pulled up a couple doors down and looked over at it. The whole street was low rent, and there were some trailers. A couple of them looked to have been there for years, added on over and over so now they resembled a hodgepodge of materials. Lawns were overgrown behind wire-mesh fences, where dogs roamed the front yards. A couple of Labradoodles barked at them.

"I'm going to talk to this woman. I want you to come in with me."

Liberty sniffed and smoothed back her hair. "Okay."

Her voice was small, like he'd kicked her cat. Which he would never do, even though it was seriously freaky to hang out in the same room as a hairless cat. He didn't particularly want to push her when she was hurt and upset, but the idea of facing his niece kind of terrified him. What if this was his only shot at a family, through his brother's child, and he messed it up the way he'd evidently messed up his relationship with Liberty? Tate didn't know if he'd be able to handle that on top of everything else, including the threat of criminal charges against him.

They walked down the sidewalk together, neither touching nor saying anything. Tate hated this tension. Sure, a huge part of him still had feelings for her. Probably even loved her. But he simply wasn't done grieving the loss of what they'd had.

And likely, neither was she.

Which meant this whole spending-time-together thing probably wasn't good for either of them.

Liberty stood to the side while Tate knocked on the door. She was exhausted after the crying jag in the car, which—added to the lack of sleep last night after her long day of traveling—made her feel like a wet rag. She probably looked about as good as one, too. Her eyes were hot and puffy, any makeup she'd been wearing long gone now.

Tate cocked his head in her direction. Ugh. If she'd known how it felt just having him train that gaze she'd loved on her, she never would've come. She didn't regret being here, but she hadn't prepared herself for how much it was going to *hurt*. Or the fact that he was going to ask questions.

Good thing she was never, ever going to tell him why she'd broken up with him.

He'd tell her she was wrong. He'd fight for them, and he'd probably win her over. Because that was Tate. Of course he would convince her staying together was the right thing. It was why she had to stand strong and fight the feeling that seemed to pull them together like magnets. If she gave in she would spend the rest of her life waiting for the moment he realized he'd stayed when he should have moved on.

No, thank you.

The door swung open. Natalie Stand was a slender woman who wore jeans and a tank top. She stood in the doorway, a chubby toddler on her hip. Despite having a heavy hand with the makeup brush, the woman was beautiful—Francis had been right about that. Her hair cascaded in loose curls that the baby had a handful of, strands of brown, gold and caramel. It was so pretty Liberty nearly gasped. Then she ran a hand down her own mousy blond hair, feeling even more disheveled than she had a minute ago.

The woman's penciled-on eyebrow shifted. "Can I help you?" There was a lilt of an accent, but Liberty couldn't place it.

Tate led the conversation, as they'd planned. "Natalie Stand?" When she nodded, he said, "I'm Deputy Sheriff Tate Almers, and this is Liberty Westmark. She's with the Secret Service."

The woman took a step back, whether involuntary or not. "Almers?"

Tate nodded. "Braden is my brother. He's actually why we're here."

The woman sighed. "You should come in." She led them to a living room peppered with baby toys, and Liberty spotted a couple of pacifiers. The kitchen was worn but clean, with the exception of a mug and a half-empty sippy cup on the counter. All normal stuff. There were books, magazines and DVDs on the unit by the TV, and a few pairs of shoes by the front door—some women's shoes, plus boots and sneakers, the kind a man would wear. A man with much bigger feet than Natalie.

She heard the toddler make some indecipherable noises then move off toward the TV. Tate had Natalie talking about how she and Braden had met, like this was a friendly chat. Liberty continued to study the room. The couches and coffee table. The ceiling.

A tiny hand touched the arm of the couch beside her. Liberty stiffened.

Tate paused, midsentence. He might have looked at her. Probably frowned. Liberty didn't look at him.

The tiny girl rounded the couch and bumped into Liberty's knee.

She couldn't move.

Curly blond hair. The girl started and glanced up at Liberty, surprised she was on the couch. A war played across her face—smile at the new person, or cry because she had no idea who Liberty was and why she was there. Braden's nose—Tate had the same one—wrinkled on her face. The eyes were similar, set deep into her tiny face. She was beautiful, clearly Braden's daughter… and Tate's niece.

"Liberty?"

She started at his voice. The little girl took a breath and started to cry. Natalie swooped her up. "I'm sorry. She's usually such a people person."

Liberty tried to smile, but it felt false even to her. "That's okay," she choked out. "She's sweet." And Liberty was a liar. It hadn't been okay since she'd quit serving in the children's ministry at church. She hadn't even been able to look at a stroller since, and here God had asked her to face Tate's niece. It shouldn't feel like a slap in the face, but what was she supposed to think?

God had promised to give her the desires of her heart, hadn't he? But no. That wasn't her lot to enjoy in life. Liberty had nothing she wanted, and the lack of anything real she could call "hers" screamed at her every second of every day. But now wasn't the time to dissolve into a fit of crying over the unfairness of it all. They were supposed to be interviewing Natalie.

Liberty mustered up as much willpower as she could and straightened. She looked at Natalie without letting her gaze stray to the little girl, now sucking on a hank of her mom's hair. "Do you know of any dealings Braden may have had with locals of Russian descent?"

Natalie sat, and as she did so, Liberty realized it was a delay tactic. Settling herself and her daughter onto the couch took a moment, and she used it to compose herself and carefully craft her answer.

"Russians?" She blew out a breath, like she was thinking intently. "I don't know. He isn't here that much, and I don't know everyone he hangs out with."

"He doesn't live here?"

"No," Natalie said with a frown.

Tate had a *get it together* look on his face. "Ms. Stand already answered that question." He turned to the woman across from them. "Any idea where Braden might be now?"

Natalie shook her head.

"How about where he was last night?"

"Didn't you say he was with Russians?"

Liberty said, "Just that he was found at the house this morning."

"I have no idea where Braden sleeps on a regular basis, except for his apartment. He's here maybe every couple of weeks, give or take. Usually drops off money, mooches some dinner off me and once in a while hangs out with Tasha so I can go out with my friends." Natalie sighed. "It's not perfect, but it works for me. Tasha and I don't need that kind of dysfunction in our lives. It's too disrupting having to deal constantly with a toddler and a man who acts like one."

Liberty nodded. The one time she'd met Braden there had been glimpses of that, even when he was relatively sober. "How do you get ahold of him?"

Natalie shrugged. "I have his number."

Liberty glanced at Tate, who said, "Maybe you could give it to me."

Good, he hadn't already asked that question, so she didn't look like a total idiot. Again. Tate was probably going to ask her what had happened later. Questions she wouldn't want to answer almost as much as she hadn't wanted to answer questions about their breakup.

Natalie scrolled through her cell phone protected by a sparkly pink case, and then read off some numbers to Tate.

Liberty always assumed people knew more than they thought they did. At least, that had been her experience. So she said, "Think back to the last time he was here for a second. What time of day was it?"

Natalie didn't look impressed by the question. "Dinnertime, I guess. I was feeding Tasha cereal when he showed up."

"How long did he stay?"

"Long enough I had to make twice as much chicken as I'd planned."

"And he ate with you?"

Natalie nodded. Tate sat silently, letting Liberty ask the questions. Her next was, "What did you talk about?"

Natalie's eyes widened. "Actually we did have a conversation. Which was weird, because it's usually awkward since there isn't much to talk about. This time he stayed longer, and we talked about the old gym in Havertown that's closing. He used to be a member there, and he really liked it. He was bummed it was shutting down."

Liberty figured it was probably nothing, but on the off chance it could turn out to be something, she would accept it. She glanced at Tate. "Havertown?"

"Thirty miles, maybe. It's a smaller town." Tate was

quiet for a moment. "Lots of places closing down because we have all the ski hills and vacation lodging, and their tourist trade isn't much to speak of."

That was probably why he wanted to sell his cabin. Make some money. Move on. The idea of it made her want to cry. She was never selling her condo. Liberty was going to die a spinster Secret Service agent, completely miserable even while being lauded for being strong and independent because she didn't need a man to take care of her.

Tate said, "Thank you for your time, Natalie."

Havertown might be nothing, but it was a potential lead at least. They stepped outside and started walking to the truck.

"I'm not even going to ask what that was with the kid," Tate said. "She did look like Braden, though."

Liberty nodded. She couldn't speak.

"And Natalie was lying."

"Maybe," Liberty managed to say.

They walked up to the Secret Service SUV, and the window on the passenger side rolled down.

"She was lying," Francis said, not looking any happier than Liberty felt.

Tate nodded. "I think she knows exactly where Braden is."

# THIRTEEN

Something was seriously going on with Liberty. As Francis talked, Tate tried to gauge what on earth it could be. She'd freaked out in Natalie's house, but Liberty liked kids and was good with people. Maybe it was him. Or he was just taking it too personally, and Liberty was just having a bad day—she'd been shot, after all—and she needed a nap.

*He* needed a nap, for that matter.

"…keep tabs on her. I'll have Intelligence dig deeper into her life as well. Find out if she has reason to hide your brother from us."

Tate realized he hadn't heard much of what Francis said. The agent in the passenger seat—Francis was driving, probably because he had to be in control all the time—smirked at Tate. He ignored Mr. Silent Opinion, and nodded to Francis.

"If she knows where her boyfriend is, we'll find out soon enough."

"And the search for the missing people?"

Francis said, "We're looking at a lot of possible places. We're stretched thin, but if there's something to be found then we're gonna find it."

A niggling thought edged into his brain. Tate wanted to grasp at it, figure out what was pinging on his radar. Something about the missing people. The videos? Their locations? It was a puzzle for him to solve, which on most days he'd have been happy to sit and mull over. Too bad that wasn't even an option right now. He'd have to make do with thinking about it while they ran down the leads they had.

Liberty said, "What about this abandoned gym in Havertown she mentioned?"

She looked so small, her face still paler than it should've been as she stood there with her arm hugging her body. The woman needed food and rest. Probably painkillers as well, though those were in the truck. Something to bring some pink to those cheeks and give her a bit of energy.

"Could be something. Could be nothing." Francis shrugged.

Tate said, "We'll check it out."

Liberty turned to him, her nose scrunched up. Tate stared her down. It was likely enough the abandoned gym would turn out to be nothing but a wild-goose chase, and Liberty would get a couple hours' reprieve from danger and stress. It sounded like the perfect assignment for them so the feds could concentrate on the most pertinent things and not waste time following dead ends.

They could get something to eat on the way, and Liberty could nap on the drive.

"Okay," Francis said. "We'll be on your tail the whole time, making sure everything's okay."

Which totally missed the point of reassigning resources to where they were best spent. Evidently Francis wasn't yet willing to let go of the idea that he could find whoever was involved by following Tate around. At least Locke and Alana were putting their focus where it would hopefully get real results.

Tate was willing to accept anything positive at this point. Those people were probably terrified they were going to be killed. "What about the ransom demand?"

Francis looked at his watch. "The US Attorney is taking care of the paperwork. He'll field it back to me when we're ready to move." He didn't look too worried about the looming deadline.

Tate did not share the man's lack of agitation. Still, he tapped the frame of the car window with his knuckles. "Then we'll be on our way."

Francis nodded, and Tate led Liberty to the sheriff's truck with one hand on the small of her back.

"Are you protecting me? You know I'm the Secret Service agent, right?"

Tate heard the amusement in her voice. "I guess old habits die hard."

Kind of like loving her and wanting to protect her. No one brought out those feelings in him but Liberty. If she just said the word, he would flip that protective switch back to on, and she would never have to worry about anything for the rest of their lives.

He glanced aside at her. Would she ever say the word and give him the signal that meant they were right back to the way they used to be? This time it would be new. They were different, they'd survived the last year apart and it had made them both stronger. The question was whether that strength could be part of their new relationship. He needed Liberty to give him some kind of sign, and then he could find out.

But, sign or not, until she told him the real reason she'd broken up with him, Tate had to wait. He had to know why she'd felt the need to cause both of them so much pain before he could open up his heart and let her in once more. Not to mention giving her the power to tear his heart out all over again.

Tate didn't like giving away any power, but that was what love was. Love meant giving up safety, security and any plans for the future, and putting them into someone else's hands. He'd been fully prepared to do that before. While Liberty, apparently, had not.

Tate hit the closest drive-through and got them both some fast food, and then watched for rogue semitrucks as he drove to the gym Natalie had mentioned. The Secret Service SUV followed from a distance, their surveillance equipment probably still active. If Francis was looking for Tate to slip up and expose his guilt, then the man was probably listening to everything. Including that conversation earlier, where Liberty had been crying.

She was asleep now, her tummy full of fatty foods she probably wouldn't have eaten if she had her wits about her. But the calories would do her good.

Tate pulled off the freeway and up to the light. He dug out his phone and tried the number Natalie had given him for Braden.

It rang and rang, and finally went to voice mail. It was a generic message, where the person hadn't taken the time to set up their own voice mail. He sighed and tossed the phone in his cup holder. It hit his soda cup and bounced down by his feet.

The light went green. Tate pushed the phone behind his shoe just so it didn't slide under the pedal and cause him to crash the truck.

It was hard to believe his brother was involved in this. He'd always thought there was a kind of injustice to the fact that Braden hated him so badly. The kid had this tendency to take things too personally, and the adult he'd grown into wasn't much different. Still, it was a big leap from moody kid to a man intent on destroying the lives of three people and framing his brother for it. Taking down a plane was a huge undertaking.

There had to be someone else behind it. It couldn't be Braden alone.

Tate couldn't help thinking all this was serving to thoroughly distract the Secret Service. Even with some out searching for the plane, too many others—like Francis back there in his SUV—were entirely focused on Tate.

What if it was all a smoke screen?

Could there possibly be more to this than what they already knew? Tate didn't know what it might be, but he wanted to get to his brother and find out. Braden had to know. Or the Russians knew. If Tate could find their head boss, the one who called all the shots, he'd be one step closer to finding out.

One step closer to knowing why they were so intent on framing him as the prime suspect.

Liberty opened her eyes. The truck was stopped, and they were in a parking lot. Everything was still covered in snow, but she could live the dream—the one where it was eighty and she was drinking an iced soda with nothing to do but watch the sweat of condensation run down the outside of the glass.

In most of those dreams, Tate was right there beside her. He'd always looked good sporting a nice tan. She turned to him then, the subject of all the dreams she'd just been having. He was still in that giant coat, and in the credit union she'd noticed that his beard had hints of red coloring. She'd always loved his smile. When he was asleep, he never had that scowl on his face.

Liberty sighed.

"Feel better?"

"Actually, I do." She tried to stretch in the cab of the truck as much as she could without moving one arm. "Thank you for the food. And the nap time."

He nodded and Liberty took stock of the situation. None of her pressing problems had gone away. Eventually she'd have to see a doctor about her arm. It was manageable most of the time, but if she moved wrong, her shoulder screamed murder at her to quit it. However, she felt better. Not well enough she wanted to have another long conversation that ended in tears. Just well enough she was the first out of the car.

The building had been a full complex gym, with an Olympic-sized pool and everything. Now it just looked sad. The windows were busted, probably from kids with rocks or baseballs. The front doors were boarded up, and the sign that hung on the outside wall was missing a couple of letters. The rest of the letters were dusted with snow.

Tate rounded the hood of the truck.

"Hopefully it doesn't take too long to search this whole place," she said. He didn't seem to mind, though. His attention was on the SUV that had followed them from Natalie's house. Liberty looked over. No one got out.

"Guess we're on our own in there." Tate sighed.

"I'm sure we can handle it."

His lips twitched. "Sure, so long as the weight of snow on the roof hasn't compromised it. If it hasn't fallen in by now, it could collapse on top of us while we're inside."

"Wow. Such a happy thought."

They trudged across the snow-covered grass between the cars and the building. It was maybe ten feet at most. Liberty glanced back at the men in the SUV, just sitting there watching them do all the work. She knew she and Tate were on the cakewalk assignment, and she was fine with it. It was no secret she wasn't up to her normal operating level. In fact, she was far from it. She was going to need a vacation from her vacation when this trip was done. Not that this was either a vacation or an assignment—not with all that had happened. But it was almost Christmas, so that could be her *real* vacation.

She stumbled on something buried under the snow, and Tate caught her good arm.

"Okay?"

She nodded, too embarrassed to say anything. The part of her dream that wasn't set on the beach had been an extended Christmas montage where she and Tate drank eggnog, watched old movies like they'd done so many times and decorated a tree. They even walked the dogs in the snow, then returned home for hot chocolate. Food always featured prominently in her dreams, and it didn't matter if she was on a beach or in his beautiful Christmas cabin.

She couldn't believe he was selling it.

Liberty pushed aside those unhelpful dreams. It wouldn't do her any good to get more caught up in them than she had been. She surveyed the area instead, looking for any sign of life. It was midafternoon, so she'd figured kids might be running around the place getting up to trouble. Or maybe they were good at not getting caught.

None of the sidewalks around the place had been shoveled. She didn't even know where the sidewalks *were* underneath the snow, but it meant she could tell that no one had been here since the last snowfall. No footprints.

"You really like this weather?"

"Sure."

"Mostly I figure people are lying when they say that, because you can't possibly enjoy being this freezing." She glanced at him. "Can you?"

"I like it, Lib."

"Do you ski?" Aside from growing up here, there had to be a reason he liked winter enough to live in this part of Montana, where the snow was hip-height and her nose was numb. Did he like breathing in icicles and feeling like his legs were going to freeze solid?

"I ski a little." He studied her, like he was trying to figure her out. "You?"

"You know I don't." They'd never been skiing. They'd never even talked about it. She frowned at him. "And why would I do that in favor of lying on a beach, soaking up vitamin D and taking a nap?"

"Florida girl."

"Born and raised."

He grinned. "And now you're stuck in DC."

"I could move back if I wanted to. Or maybe I'll get stationed in Bora Bora next. That might be nice."

Tate frowned, then ran a hand through his hair. "Sure, I guess."

They circled the building with him leading the way.

Liberty ignored whatever was going on in his head and pointed out a pertinent fact. "The door was at the front."

"I know. I'm looking to see if any of the entrances have been used at all, or recently."

Oh. Why hadn't she thought of that? "I think I'm losing my edge."

"I think you've been shot. That's enough to make anyone lose their edge."

"So you're not disagreeing with me."

Tate shot her a look. "You don't have to worry about not holding up your end of things."

"But what if I miss something, and—"

"Lib," he stopped her. "I've got you covered, okay?"

"You should have sent me with those EMTs."

"You could have sent yourself."

She pressed her lips together, then said, "Touché."

Tate chuckled. He stopped at what looked like a loading dock. "This has been used recently."

Sure enough, there were tire tracks. "Truck, looks like." Someone had visited this old, abandoned gym this morning.

"Let's find a door and check it out."

Tate used his shoulder to break the lock on the door to the side of the loading dock's garage-type door. He flipped on a flashlight and held it up, his gun hand braced on his fist holding the light. Liberty held her gun up, still tucking her left arm to her body. She'd be useless in a fight, but she could still shoot straight if she needed to.

The whole place was empty. It didn't take too long to walk through and then circle back to the loading entrance.

Tate studied the floor. "Looks like something might've

been here." Sure enough, there were scratch marks. Like from pallets. "Whatever it was, it's gone now."

Liberty wandered to the door, its glass still intact and no board in place. She looked out at the other buildings. The part of the SUV she could see. Frozen trees. Rooftops.

A man settling a giant tube-shaped device onto his shoulder.

Aimed right at them.

"Tate." She said his name on a gasp.

"What is it?" He moved toward her, but she turned and shoved him back into the center of the building. Pain screamed through her arm but she ignored it.

"Run."

"What—"

"Rocket launcher!" she screamed. "Run!"

# FOURTEEN

The words penetrated Tate's brain, and his legs kicked into gear. He wanted to go back, to give himself reason to believe what his head didn't want to comprehend.

A rocket launcher in small-town Montana? Still, he ran like his life depended on it, because it likely did.

He would get hit if he went back. Liberty would get caught in it as well, or she would come back for him if he didn't move fast enough for her liking. The woman was a force to be reckoned with when she wasn't running on an injury and next to no sleep.

The explosion ripped through the building from his right, a wave of sound, then a feeling like an earthquake had split the ground. Smoke and fire rushed at them.

They reached a set of double doors and pushed through to the pool.

Tate grabbed Liberty, unable to take the time to be careful of her injury. He jumped off the edge of the empty pool into the air. The force of the explosion hit the big room. It hit them in midair, shoving Tate and Liberty toward the far end of the pool. He grabbed her as best he could and held her in front of him as he turned.

Tate's back slammed into hard tile. His head snapped back, and he blacked out amid an ocean of hot air.

He woke up sometime later. The face of his watch was cracked, the display blank where digital numbers should have told him what time it was. The room was lit by daylight, the tile of the pool black and littered with debris. Drywall dust danced in the air, and what had been the doors was now a giant hole in the wall. Twisted metal lay on sheets of broken drywall intermingled with snow. Cold air from outside now whipped through the room like it was a wind tunnel, rustling his hair.

He tried to move, but the pain in his head stalled any motion he might've been able to manage. Liberty's weight covered his torso and legs. Was she unconscious, as he had been? Tate managed to get his arm out from under him and winced at the muscles in his shoulder. He reached up and touched the hair on the back of his head. His fingertips came back wet with blood.

His phone.

Tate rummaged around for it, absently shifting Liberty. "Wake up, Lib." He didn't find his phone. Where was it?

The truck. He'd dropped it and kicked it behind his shoe, then had forgotten to bring it with him.

Tate bit down on his molars and searched Liberty's jacket pockets for her cell. When he found it and pulled it out, the screen was completely shattered. He pressed the button, but when it illuminated he couldn't even read what anything said.

He patted her arm and gently shook her. "Liberty." They were going to have to walk out of here. Provided he could put one foot in front of the other without falling over. He could hardly think through the pain. It felt like his head had been split open. There was probably a dent in the tile where he'd landed.

Liberty groaned, a long, low sound of intense pain. Tate shifted her off his legs so he could see her shoulder. Yep, she was bleeding as well.

Tate didn't want to wait, so he got his feet under him and lifted her as he rose to stand. While she blinked, Tate waited for the room to stop spinning. Then they started walking.

Where were Francis and his men? And firefighters? They needed an ambulance—now.

"Thank You, God, we aren't trapped," Tate said.

Liberty's mouth curled up. "Amen to that." She glanced around. "How are we gonna get out of here?"

Tate turned his body to look for an exit so he didn't have to turn his head.

Liberty gasped. "Tate!"

He looked back to see her whip off her coat. She winced but got her sweater off, and then put her coat back on. She balled it up. "Press this to the back of your head. I doubt you should be upright and moving around, but I don't think I can carry you out of here." She led him to the edge of the pool, and he climbed the steps. "As long as you're upright, I'm going to trust it so that we can get ourselves out of here."

Once he'd let go of the stair handle, Tate pressed the sweater to the back of his head. The touch whipped white shards across his vision like lightning. He almost blacked out, and then Liberty was under his arm with hers around his waist.

"This might be a problem." She worried her bottom lip. "But you need to keep that on there."

"Yes, ma'am."

Liberty made a tut sound with her mouth as she walked with him—slowly—toward a fire exit door at the far end of the pool area. "I did not miss that sarcasm."

Tate smiled. "I missed you."

Liberty leaned on the exit bar on the door. "Thank You, God, this whole place wasn't destroyed. Just the other end of the building." She hesitated a second. "Unless I push on this and the building comes down on us."

She glanced up at him. Tate couldn't seem to find the words to say. "Lib." He wanted to touch her cheek. Why did she look so worried?

"We can't wait. I have to risk it." She paused. "If we do get squished… I mean, we almost died already, but if we die now… I missed you. No matter what happens, I don't think that will ever change."

Tate loved hearing that, because he felt the same way. "Missed you, too, Lib." The words were kind of mumbled. When he leaned in to kiss her, the room started spinning.

"Whoa." She shifted under him. Tate's body moved without him intending it to. His shoulder hit the exit bar, and the door opened. They stumbled through, but Liberty got under his shoulder and lifted his body back upright like a professional.

Cold air whipped his face and clothes. It was entirely too light outside, so he shut his eyes. Snow crept into his boots as they walked.

"You're strong," he grunted. Which wasn't all he wanted to say, but it was all he could get out.

"Yeah, well." She groaned out the words. "It turns out there's a lot of free time for strength training when you don't have a life or any friends."

"I'm your friend."

"Yes, Tate." There was a smile in her voice. "You are."

A police siren sounded close by. Tate groaned. "Too loud."

"It's Dane."

The sheriff said, "Sit down?"

"Yes, that's probably a good idea. He's really hurt, Dane. He's slurring his words." She lowered him into the snow and took the sweater. Did she need it? No, Liberty put it under his head. Then she yelled, "He needs an ambulance!"

Was he really that hurt? Tate tried to open his eyes, to get a look at her face, but nothing seemed to be working.

"It's on the way." Dane was quiet for a second, but then his footsteps got closer. "You don't look so good either, Liberty."

Worry permeated Tate's body like a cold frost, and he shivered, then reached for her hand. Was she okay?

"I'll go with him and get checked out myself when I know he's okay."

Dane didn't say anything for a while.

"Dane?"

"Yeah, Tate. I'm here."

Tate didn't open his eyes. Liberty said, "You're the only one here?"

"Help is on the way."

"What about the Secret Service? Their SUV was around that side, behind where we parked your truck."

Tate was glad she asked; he didn't seem to be able to make more than one or two words.

"There are two fire trucks over there that just got here," Dane said. "Not much left of my truck you guys were driving. The one parked behind it was flipped over. They're cutting the agents out now."

"What?" Tate snapped his eyes open. Too bright. He tried to sit up. Pain snapped through his skull like he'd been hit with a lightning rod. "They…"

Blackness rushed in from the edges of his vision and swallowed him whole.

"We need that ambulance!"

Dane touched her shoulder, but she shrugged him off. Tate's eyes had rolled back in his head, and then his whole body had gone limp. "He'll be okay, Liberty."

"You didn't see the back of his head." What if he needed surgery? What if his brain was bleeding?

Dane motioned to the vehicle as it pulled up. "There they are."

It took forever for them to climb out of their ambulance and race over. "He hit his head in the explosion." She didn't want to move away, but they needed room to get Tate on their backboard.

Dane helped her stand. "You okay?"

No, she wasn't okay. Her shoulder smarted more than she thought possible, but she pushed aside the pain to focus on what was happening.

"Update me," she said.

Dane didn't look convinced, but she saw the moment he decided to acquiesce. Liberty desperately needed to feel like she had a handle on this situation. It was so out of control.

"The fire department is cutting the agents out of their car. One is dead—"

"Francis?"

"Which one is he?"

"The driver."

"Then no," Dane said. "It was the passenger who was killed in the explosion. The driver and the two who were in the back seat are alive, but I don't know much more than that."

Liberty blew out a breath.

"They have some pretty bad injuries. All of them are unconscious. We'll have to see what the doctors say." Dane paused. "You're going with Tate, right?"

She glanced at the two EMTs. One said, "That's a nasty crack on the back of his head."

Liberty nodded, unable to say anything without dissolving into painful tears. She swallowed and looked at Dane. "Yes, I'm going with Tate. But you need to find Natalie Stand, because she told us to come here. And when we did?" Liberty swept her arm to encompass the building in its now disastrous state.

Dane nodded. "I'll pick her up."

Liberty fisted her hands by her sides. "I don't understand." The thoughts had barely coalesced in her mind, and she had no idea what they meant, but she needed to talk it through with *someone*. "Why shoot up this place? Isn't that a little obvious?" She paused. "They'll never get their money or the guy released from prison if the agents they're dealing with are in the hospital."

"So they were aiming for you and Tate, and the other Secret Service agents got caught in the cross fire?"

Liberty glanced around, trying to work it out. "Maybe. I mean, it's sloppy. They must not have known exactly who was in the SUV. And if Tate and I were the targets, why kill us? Doing that won't convince the Secret Service Tate was behind it. Not unless they're still trying to pin it on him, making it look like he's guilty even while he's helping solve this." That didn't explain things, though.

"The feds still don't know where those people are."

Liberty shook her head. "We have to find them."

Dane shot her a dark look. "I know that. I've been looking at the locations but nothing is jumping out at me as a possibility for where they might head next."

"We don't have an address for the ransom delivery?"

Dane shook his head. "If they keep to their timeline so far, there will be one more video before the ransom."

"And if they kill the first hostage during that live broadcast?"

"Let's pray they don't."

Could she do that? Could Liberty trust God with something so important when she'd spent the last year bemoaning the fact that He hadn't trusted her with something as important as having a future of her own? There was a mental block between her and letting God have full control of her life once again. As though she'd trusted Him with everything, and in return He hadn't done the same.

One of the EMTs called out, "Let's go."

She spun to watch the EMT lift Tate onto a backboard. His head had been secured, which made him look worse. A whimper worked its way up her throat. What if he died? He might not be in her life anymore, but if this injury killed him, she didn't know what she would do. She was already living only halfway, surviving but not thriving as she had when she'd been secure in their relationship and had God's goodness in her life. Now all she had was herself, and mostly it was just lonely.

"Go with them," Dane said.

He walked her to the ambulance and helped her in.

Just before he shut the doors, he said to the EMT, "She needs to see a doctor as well."

The EMT shot her a look, like she'd disappointed him.

Liberty said, "That was the plan, okay?" She leaned her head back against the side of the ambulance and closed her eyes. The door shut, and the vehicle pulled out. For the first time in a long time, Liberty prayed. She asked for protection for both her and Tate, healing for him and help for those agents. Some of them would likely end up in intensive care for a while. Then she prayed the people behind all this would be caught.

While Tate got an MRI to make sure there was no bleeding in his brain, Liberty saw a doctor and got stitched up. The doctor wasn't too happy about the fact that she spent the whole time he was working on her on the phone with Locke. But the clock on the wall ticked closer and closer to the deadline for the release of the man from federal prison. A man they had learned was Venezuelan.

"You know we're not actually going to let him out, right?" Locke asked the question carefully.

Of course she knew that. She'd just never been in a hostage/ransom situation before. "You're not even going to consider the fact that three people might die if you don't?"

"They know the drill, and so do you." That didn't mean she had to like it. "We're looking everywhere for them. The locations picked were very specific. Wi-Fi they could hack, after hours. No people."

"It's Saturday. What location has Wi-Fi and is closed right now?"

"Aside from that credit union?" Locke said. "A handful of places. We're hitting each one, and we'll cross them all off before the deadline, so let's pray we find them."

"I will." Especially if it meant those people didn't lose their lives.

"How's Tate?"

"I'll know for sure when his test results come in. They said that the fact that he hasn't woken up yet doesn't necessarily mean anything."

Locke sighed audibly. "Okay."

"Find those people, Locke."

"Stay safe, Liberty."

She hung up, and the doctor shot her a pointed look but tied off the stitches. He could glare all he wanted, but she had work to do regardless of whether she'd been shot or not. He released her, and she sat in the waiting area.

Tate was wheeled to a room, and she sat with him. They'd bandaged his head, which made him look frail even though he was so big. He'd always been so strong. Protective.

Liberty brushed her hand over his cheek and sat by his elbow. "Wake up."

She didn't know what she would say to him if he did, but she just wanted to see the blue of his eyes. She wanted to see the way he looked at her, tell him she'd always loved him, even from the first moment they met. He wasn't like any other man she'd ever known. Some people might think that his independence was a problem because it caused him to butt heads with others, but she knew it was the thing that made him special. Strong enough to withstand everything he already had and still have the courage to go his own way, Tate had forged a path all his own.

Liberty wanted to soak up that strength. Maybe borrow it for a while so she could finally tell him why she'd broken up with him. She choked back a sob. Maybe one day he would even understand why she'd told him to move on without her, maybe even say he'd have done the same thing.

As Liberty watched the slow rise and fall of his chest, she couldn't help thinking how much she'd missed just being around him. The people trying to kill him had nearly succeeded. She'd nearly lost the man she loved.

What was she going to do about that, just sitting here staring at him? She couldn't have him. He would never accept her back, but she could help him to live more fully.

Tate's eyes started to flutter. A low moan issued from deep in his throat.

Liberty rushed out of the room before he saw her.

# FIFTEEN

"I'm afraid I'm going to have to advise you not to leave, sir."

Tate didn't look at the doctor. He was concentrating on putting his arms in the scrubs top they'd given him. "You said the test indicated everything was good."

"Doesn't mean there isn't a hole in the back of your head."

"Don't worry, Doc, I'll wait an hour before I go swimming." Maybe that wasn't intended for a head injury, but the doctor would get the idea he planned to be safe. Tate wanted to know where Liberty was. No one had answered their phones, and he'd thought for sure she would be here with him when he woke up.

Instead he'd been greeted by an empty room and the fog he figured was from whatever they'd given him to kill the pain in his head. *Thank You, God, for modern medicine.*

Finally he'd gotten through to Dane, who was coming to pick him up.

The doctor sighed. "I don't even know what to say to that."

"Whatever I need to sign, I'll sign." Tate shrugged

on his jacket, which was still damp, and sat on the edge of the bed. "But I gotta get out of here."

The doctor moved to the door. "I'll have an orderly bring a wheelchair. You are not walking out of here. No strenuous activity, and I'd advise you to curtail anything except for lying down as much as you possibly can. Any symptoms of disorientation, dizziness, blackouts or anything else at all and I want you back here, no complaints."

"Done."

Fifteen minutes later, Dane pulled up at the curb, Tate's dogs in the back seat. "That's my ride."

The orderly wheeled Tate out the door and up to the sheriff's vehicle, which was good because Tate didn't think he could have made it that far on his feet. Both dogs barked. The sound split through his head. "Quiet."

They stopped, and he glanced up at Dane, whose eyes widened. "Are you sure you're not supposed to be in there still?"

Tate ignored the question. "Where's Liberty?"

"She got stitches and a prescription."

He waited for more. "And?"

Dane sighed. "I dropped her off with Director Locke."

She'd gone back to work? Tate didn't want to accept the fact that she'd chosen work over him, but it was the truth. Was that what she'd done a year ago as well?

He'd always been a realist. They'd spent a lot of time together over the past couple of days, but evidently it hadn't been enough to convince Liberty she should trust him enough to share what she was still keeping secret. It was like she wanted to punish herself for something. To suffer—and make him suffer as well.

Dane helped him into the passenger seat. She wasn't

the only one suffering, but he didn't want to think about the fact that he'd cracked his head open. Liberty was hurt as well, and yet she insisted on continuing to hurt the two of them more by being in town and refusing to answer his question.

Tate rested his elbow at the bottom of the window, made a fist and leaned his head against it. She should never have come here if she wasn't going to actually talk to him. Really talk. She thought she was helping, but Liberty just didn't understand the fact that he couldn't handle small talk when there was so much more to say. Things that actually *meant* something. To both of them.

"Are you really okay?"

Tate looked at Dane out of the corner of his eye. "Just tell me where we're going."

"Last on the list of locations with Wi-Fi," Dane said. "In other news, Natalie Stand is gone. The daughter was with a neighbor when I knocked on doors seeing if anyone knew where she was. They all said she's private, but also that she frequently has male visitors, and only occasionally it's your brother."

"What is that supposed to mean?"

"It could be something other than what you're thinking. But the neighbors all said the same thing. Natalie has a varied social life, but she's a good mother. One of the neighbors said 'competent.'"

If she wasn't neglecting Tasha, at least it was something.

"There's more," Dane said. "One of the neighbors reported a late-night argument with a visitor. And get this—apparently they were yelling in Russian.

"Natalie Stand doesn't exist except for a driver's license and the birth record for Natasha Stand. She has a rental agreement, utilities. But nothing else. No birth certificate for Mom, or where she went to school. After the neighbor told me he heard Russian from one of her visitors I followed a hunch. Found a sealed juvenile record in Chicago for a Natalia Standovich. First driver's license photo she's a purple-haired sixteen-year-old, but it's her."

"So she came here to start over?" Tate said. "Maybe the Russians found her. Like her past caught up with her."

"Maybe." Dane didn't sound convinced. "The BOLO is out, and there's a deputy sitting on her street in case she comes back."

Tate wanted to nod but he was trying to avoid moving his head at all. "If she'd run, she would've taken Tasha." He couldn't believe he hadn't seen the signs that Natalie had been hiding her Russian heritage. She might have just moved on from the life, but it was also possible it hadn't severed all ties with her. Natalie—or Natalia rather—might be as involuntarily caught up in this as Tate was.

"Locke and his team are headed to the same place we are. The last place on the list they think those three people might be."

"They're probably on the road in a van."

The videos were made on brief stop-offs. Tate wasn't convinced they would find those people in time. Whoever was behind this wanted a Venezuelan released from jail and had a working relationship with the Russians. "If they keep them mobile it's harder to find them because they're constantly on the go. It's what I'd do."

"Then let's pray they aren't as smart as you."

Dane parked just down the street from the library. The parking lot was full of vehicles, state police and government SUVs. The front door was open, and agents in vests were stationed by the door.

"They must have breached already."

He cracked his door and listened to the far-off cries of, "Clear!" Then finally the last call came. "Found them!"

Tate crossed the parking lot with Dane. The Secret Service agent on the door was a former colleague. The man lifted his chin but said nothing as Tate stepped inside.

At least fifteen agents filled the small-town library. On the cushioned chairs in the center sat the missing people: Edward Frampton, Bethany Piers and Anthony Wills. All three were tied up and gagged. The agents began to assist in untying them. Across the room Director Locke had a man facedown on the floor. His knee was planted in the middle of the man's back as he secured the guy.

Tate looked around for Liberty.

"I'm surprised you're out of the hospital. I heard you hit your head pretty hard." The female agent motioned to the bandage wrapped around his head.

"It's the latest fashion, you know?" When she cracked a smile, he asked, "Alana, right?"

"Alana Preston." They shook hands.

"You caught the guy holding these people?"

She nodded. "Not sure he's the head of the snake, as it were. But at least we're one step closer."

"Any idea where Liberty is, Alana?"

"Agent Westmark wasn't part of the breach due to her injuries. She waited outside by the vehicle."

"I didn't see her outside." He frowned, but it hurt his head. Tate turned and found Dane still behind him.

"You okay, buddy?"

"Where's Liberty?" He didn't like not knowing where she was. When this was done, she would leave with her team and take his heart with her. Still, she had to be safe and alive in order to live the life she wanted.

He strode to the door and scanned the outside.

Where was Liberty?

She planted her feet, but the man continued to drag her down the street.

Liberty had tried everything to get away. All because she'd been an idiot and actually *hidden* when she'd seen Tate and Dane show up. She was such a chicken she couldn't even face him. He was out of the hospital! She'd been torn between rushing over to help him, and what had been her final decision—crouching behind a car so he didn't see her.

That was where this guy had found her. Hoodie pulled so low over his head it cast his face into shadows, he'd hit her with a stun gun. Liberty moved at the last second, so the blast wasn't full force. She'd managed not to black out, but her legs crumpled and she'd hit the ground.

Then he felt around her. What on earth was he...? The man pulled out her gun and tossed it aside. So that's what he'd been doing. *Thank You, Jesus.* She tried not to think about what could've happened when he hauled her to her feet.

Liberty swayed, and he grabbed her. The wound in her shoulder pulled like the stitches were going to rip out. She tried to scream, but no sound came out of her mouth. The stun gun's effects made her brain fuzzy, but she could still think. She just couldn't do anything, or say anything. This man was going to take her away, and no one would know where she was.

She wanted to scream that she was being kidnapped and alert someone to what was happening. Tate was here. Why wasn't he saving her?

The man dragged her to his car, all the while muttering and cursing about how heavy she was. Excuse her for enjoying a doughnut sometimes. He didn't have to be mean about it.

Maybe Tate wasn't going to come. She'd have to get herself out of this.

Liberty gathered herself enough to finally be able to cry out. And she did. She screamed like her life depended on it—which she figured it likely did. She hadn't liked the feeling of not being able to speak at all, which added more volume and frustration to her fearful cry. The man slapped a hand over her mouth, muting the scream.

Liberty bit the hand.

He cried out and slapped her across the face. His grip on her never loosened, no matter how much she struggled to get away. Who was he?

"Let me go!" she yelled.

*Please, God. Let someone hear me.*

He lifted her off her feet and she flung her legs all over the place, trying to kick him. The man shifted her, then all of a sudden let go. Just dropped her. Liberty fell on her rump on the sidewalk. She cried out when pain shot up her spine.

Boots pounded the pavement, but she didn't have time to turn around. The man's body jerked, ready to run.

"Don't think about it, Braden."

Tate's brother?

Liberty sighed with relief that Tate was here. He'd heard her.

She shifted on the ground and found Tate and Dane both behind her, guns drawn. Tate was so good-looking. She tried to remember why it had been so important to leave him at the hospital, all alone, instead of staying and taking care of him.

Adrenaline bled from her muscles, and her shoulder sagged. Neither of them looked at her. "Hey, guys." She gave them a little wave. "Nice to see you."

Dane chuckled. "You okay down there, Liberty?" He asked the question as he stepped past her and cuffed Tate's brother.

Tate had a bandage around his head and looked as in need of a nap as she was.

She said, "Should you be out of the hospital?"

He held out one hand to her, his dark gaze on his brother. Liberty didn't pull on it too much and got to her feet using mostly her own steam. He ignored her question. "What just happened?"

"Well, I was—"

"Not you," Tate cut her off. "Braden."

Dane pulled him closer to Tate, and Liberty slipped around behind him. She was hiding from his brother, but she'd had a hard day. Liberty wanted to sit down. Instead she hugged Tate's waist from behind and leaned her forehead on the back of his coat. It was still damp. And cold. But the chill injected some life into her cloudy brain and woke her up a bit.

"Well?" Tate said. He shifted his arm so it held up her bad one, taking the weight off her wound.

Liberty didn't look around him at his brother. She

just listened as Braden said, "Look…I don't know what I was doing."

"You were kidnapping her."

"I was helping!"

The sheriff made a scoffing noise. Tate's whole body stiffened. "Explain."

"They're trying to kill you guys. I had to get Liberty away from it, so I figured if I just stunned her and found a place to stick her until it blew over then she'd be good."

"She's a Secret Service agent, Braden, with a team to protect her. Not to mention me." Her heart swelled. Even if she didn't want to accept it, she had help. A family of people around her who were ready to close in if she needed them. She only had to ask.

"You're not up to it," Braden said. "You got blown up."

Tate shifted. "Who wants her dead?"

"You know who."

"You work for the Russians?"

"It's more complicated than that."

"Where is Natalia Standovich?"

Braden sucked in a breath. "How do you know about her?"

"I know a lot of things," Tate said. "Like the fact that you have a daughter."

"So?"

Tate repeated his brother's word. "So."

"What does it matter if I have a kid?"

Liberty swallowed. More people approached, which meant she needed to let go of Tate. She shifted away from his back, though she wanted more than anything to just live there. Maybe forever. Ugh. Why did he have to make her feel like this when no other man ever had?

If he were anyone else, she could have walked away. Her reasoning would be the same, but it wouldn't hurt this much. The pain was tangible.

Tate shifted and clasped her right hand. "Not so fast," he whispered. "Not again."

Locke strode over. "What's going on?"

It was Dane who answered. "I'm taking Braden in. Attempted kidnapping."

Locke lifted one brow and glanced at her. Liberty nodded. The director said, "We'll follow you and bring the guy we have from the library. Are you set up to question two suspects separately?"

"Sure thing," Dane said. "Whatever you guys need."

"Did you find them?"

Locke glanced at her. "Yes. We rescued the missing three people, Agent Westmark. They're safe now."

Tate shook his head. "I still think it's a smoke screen for something else."

Beyond him, Liberty watched Braden smirk.

She said, "You know what it is."

Braden shrugged. "So what if I do?"

He'd just tried to kidnap her—even if he claimed it was to protect her—so she didn't particularly want to talk to him. But she needed to. Liberty put on her "agent" face, and said, "If you do, then you can tell us how to stop it. Tell us who you work for…or, better yet, help us bring down the whole operation."

Braden paled. "I don't…"

"That's not going to happen," Tate said. "We're not trusting him, Lib. He just tried to kidnap you. Braden doesn't come near you ever again, or he's going to have more serious problems than the load he has right now."

"What?" She pulled on his hand instead of setting it on her hip so he knew she meant business.

"No way, Lib. I'm not letting go."

"Braden can help us." Tate wasn't worried his brother would get hurt, was he? "He can be the bait in our trap to bring them down."

"There's no way my brother's being bait. He'll sell us all out and pocket the cash on the deal."

"It's our only option for—"

"The answer's no, Liberty."

Director Locke said, "Actually, it's a good idea." He looked proud of her, in a weird way. It wasn't a look she'd seen more than a handful of times. "Let's do it."

# SIXTEEN

"Don't doubt yourself now, Agent Westmark," Locke said. "Your instincts are right on."

Pride for Liberty, and how good she was at her job, swelled in Tate despite the fact that he didn't think this was a good idea at all. She looked nervous. Tate tugged on her hand so she'd move closer to him, so she could feel him beside her as she carried on the conversation with her boss.

Out of the corner of his eye, Tate saw Dane's attention was on him. The sheriff had better focus more on making sure Braden didn't get loose. He might have his hands cuffed behind his back, but Braden was wily. He could slip away.

Tate glanced at Dane and saw the man smile. Tate shook his head at whatever the sheriff was thinking. It became apparent when Dane motioned to Tate's hold on Liberty with a lift of his chin.

Tate shrugged one shoulder. Whatever pain obliterator he'd taken—painkiller was too benign for the warm numbness of what they had given him—had started to wear off. The throb at the back of his head was growing steadily more unavoidable. Kind of like a train bearing down on a car, stuck on the tracks.

No escape.

Too bad there was no time to worry about injury right now.

The conversation between Liberty and Director Locke ended, and the man walked off. Tate stepped closer to Braden. He felt Liberty flinch beside him but wasn't about to let her go. He'd done that when he'd been unconscious, and he'd woken up in the hospital to the world he'd lived in the past year. The one where she was absent, and he was completely, unavoidably alone.

There was no way he would allow that to happen again.

Braden looked everywhere but at Tate. Still, he faced down his brother. They needed information. "Was that you in those videos?"

Braden said nothing.

"He said he was me." Tate paused. "It was gonna be a different guy just now, but the one I saw looked like you." Liberty was the one who'd pointed it out, but he didn't want to draw attention to her right now. He wanted Braden's attention on him. Not on Liberty, scaring her more than she already was.

"Did you do all of the others, or just that one?" Braden still wouldn't look at him. "You're in this deep enough. You were with those prisoners at one point, which means you aren't going to be able to skirt out from under this one. Three strikes, isn't it? Means you're going away for a long time, Braden. You might as well tell me who has you involved in all this."

"And get killed in prison?" Braden's expression was incredulous. "No thanks."

"So instead you'll protect people who pull you into a threat on government personnel, like you don't know that's going to carry the maximum sentence?"

Braden's eyes were hard now. "Maybe it was my idea."

Tate tried to steel himself, but his body was just weak enough that he couldn't hold it together. "Why?" His voice was full of unshed tears.

"You're gonna cry for me now? Because I'm such a disappointment to big brother Tate, who never did anything wrong in his life."

That was what Braden thought? "Look—"

"No, you look," his brother said. "This ain't about you. Much as you want to think everything revolves around your so-much-better life."

"I'd have been fine if it didn't involve me, but I've been pulled into this at every point. They planted the flight recorder in my house, tried to kill me and Liberty—"

"I tried to stop it!"

"Because you cared so much that you needed to kidnap her?"

Braden let out a cry of frustration.

"I think you're in deep and you needed leverage. Cold feet?" Tate waited to see what reaction his brother would give him, but it didn't confirm or deny his suspicions. "Or you want to rise in the ranks so you were going to bargain your way up? Maybe secure a deal for Natalie, is that it?"

If his girlfriend was Russian, and she was perhaps on the run from her past, Braden could be involved in this as a way to secure her freedom. Oddly enough it would make Tate feel better, knowing his brother had done all this for noble reasons. At least then he would be able to understand it, instead of being completely perplexed over the fact that this man in front of him was actually his brother—his flesh-and-blood relative.

Otherwise Tate would spend the rest of his life wondering why.

But Braden gave him nothing. Not even when he was carted off to the sheriff's office to be detained.

Liberty drove the two of them in one of the Secret Service vehicles, since Tate refused to let her out of his sight. She didn't argue, but he didn't miss the look she shot him. The frown. He knew she was worried about his mental state with this head wound, but he was keeping it together. As long as the concussion didn't turn into anything more serious, he was more or less functional. He smiled to himself, then felt it leave his face. Didn't she want to stay? She'd left him at the hospital and was probably only not arguing now because he was hurt.

"Lib?"

She pulled up outside the sheriff's office and turned to him. "What?"

Her phone rang. "Hold that thought, I guess." She didn't look eager to know what he was going to say. She looked relieved.

Tate got out and waited by the hood for her to be done with her phone call, then walked inside with her. "Something important?"

She shook her head. "Doesn't matter. Are you okay?"

Tate shrugged, not feeling the need to share right now.

"Is that even the truth?"

"I'm not lying to you, Lib. The doctor gave me some things to watch out for. That's all."

She waited by the door, biting her lip.

"Come on, you guys," the desk guy said. "You're letting all the cold air in."

Tate let the door go and the man buzzed them in. Tate went straight to his desk. He sat but didn't rest his head on the back of the chair even though he wanted to. He just closed his eyes and rested his temple on his fist, his elbow on the arm of the chair.

Then someone was shaking his shoulder.

He looked up to find Liberty standing over him. She'd brushed her hair and secured it back in a ponytail. The sight of it made him smile. She was in work mode. He could handle professional Liberty, since she wasn't so hard to figure out.

"Dane and Locke are done questioning the man who held those people prisoner."

Tate nodded and stood. "How long was I out?"

"Half an hour, maybe."

He stretched. "How about you? Did you get some rest?" They both looked like they'd been through the wringer.

"We are a pair, aren't we?" She smiled. "Whoever is behind all this, we could just go scare them to death with how we look."

Tate gathered her into his arms and touched his lips to that beautiful smile of hers. "You never look bad. Even on a night like this. You're so beautiful, Liberty."

She melted into his arms, and he wasn't going to pass up the opportunity to kiss her some more. Regardless of what had happened between them, part of Tate would always belong to Liberty. And he realized then it was possible he would always love her.

Dane cleared his throat. "Uh, sorry to interrupt."

He didn't seem very sorry. Tate reluctantly turned to his friend. Dane grinned. "Time's wasting."

They followed him, despite the fact that what he'd been doing was decidedly *not* a waste of time.

Tate held Liberty's hand, ignoring the look Locke shot him. He knew how Locke felt, as the man had shared plainly his view of Tate and Liberty's relationship the day Tate quit the Secret Service. *You aren't good for her, Tate. I'm glad she broke it off, because she deserves better than a hothead like you.*

Except for the fact that it turned out it wasn't better. Not for either of them. There was a lot to resolve, but he wasn't letting Liberty go again.

Not ever.

*You're so beautiful.* Liberty hadn't been able to resist him. Not when she remembered every time he'd said that in the past. She'd call his name in the office to ask him if he wanted coffee, and he'd say, *Yeah, beautiful.* Like that was her name.

She'd loved it. And after the desert of the last year, Liberty had soaked it up like he was a fountain of fresh water. She just prayed it was going to last through what she would have to tell him. Even while she figured it was likely that he had a concussion and wasn't thinking straight.

She had to tread carefully and not lose the tiny part of what was left of her heart to him. That part she'd always kept for herself. Tate had most of it already, but she was in serious danger of just handing over the rest. Because if she had to cut off their relationship again, it would only hurt twice as badly.

"Alana checked out the phone the man had," Locke

said, all business. "It was used to make each video, and they were still stored in the phone's memory. We checked call history and text messages, but found nothing. It's clean aside from the videos, and it's unregistered." He paused. "The only thing of note is that the phone's browser was the home page for an email account. It was logged out, but we think that's how they're communicating with each other."

"Getting instructions from someone?" Liberty asked as she pushed aside everything that had just happened with Tate. They had to focus now, or this endless day of craziness would never be over. It was getting dark, and with the three hours of sleep she'd had the night before, Liberty was seriously flagging.

Locke nodded. "That's what we think. So Dane and I interviewed the man holding those people hostage, and I asked about the Venezuelan they want to be released. He claimed he had no idea who the guy was. He actually told me he'd only been with those people since earlier this afternoon."

"How can that be?"

Liberty nodded at Tate's question. She'd been about to ask the same one.

Dane answered, "I think they switched out, passed off the people they were holding and the phone to a different person every few hours. Maybe he only knew where *he* was supposed to take them and didn't know what instructions were given to the others."

"So they could've compartmentalized every part of this," Liberty said. "From the man at Tate's cabin with the flight recorder, to the ones who took us from the mine—the same ones I saw looking at the map. Then each one who was with the people they took." She paused. "And how did they get the plane on the ground, anyway?"

Locke said, "Alana spoke with the senator and the two staffers. They said the pilot was in on it. He cut the radio and then landed in a field. The men who took them were evidently supposed to pay him, but they shot the guy instead before they towed the plane into the mine."

Tate tapped the table with his fingers, a move he did when he was thinking. "I guess it's possible if they were close to the mine and they had the right equipment. I can't believe no one noticed, though."

"They said it was very early Friday morning and the sun hadn't risen yet. Though if someone saw, they're likely dead." Locke's face was grim. "These people seem to be covering their tracks well through all of this."

"And trying to frame me."

Liberty glanced at Tate. "And involving Braden. Though, maybe it was his idea to make you a part of this."

"I'll ask him," Dane said. "He's next on my list for a conversation."

Tate nodded. "I still think it's weird they tried to kill me." He glanced at her. "Us. Multiple times. Framing me is one thing, but I didn't necessarily have to be dead."

"Maybe it was because I showed up?" She thought it through, and wasn't convinced, but it was a valid suggestion. "Or they simply figured you couldn't convince anyone it wasn't true if you were dead. A deal you made that went wrong?"

Tate made a face.

Liberty thought some more. "So they draw you in, and all the Secret Service agents are so busy looking at one of their own—"

"Not anymore."

Liberty ignored his comment and said, "They wanted us looking the other way while they bargain for the release of the Venezuelan we have in prison. He could have nothing to do with this, just a name they used to ask us for something we couldn't get easily, like a van or money. Releasing someone from prison is more complicated."

"So again, they're trying to distract us?" Locke studied her like he was thinking through what she was saying. Liberty knew he respected her, but it was still nice to observe him taking her suggestions seriously.

She shrugged. "But if they really are just trying to distract us all from the search, trying to divide our focus so it takes us longer, it didn't work, did it? We found those people before the deadline, before they could make the next video."

"So we all go home," Tate said. "Job complete, everyone's headed home and the locals are tied up finishing out their investigation and dealing with the aftermath."

"You think they intended on it?" She stared at him, and he shrugged. She'd kind of figured he only kissed her because he'd hit his head and maybe he was reliving some old memories. But if he had the mental capacity to think all this through, maybe he'd been in his right mind.

He'd called her beautiful. And kissed her.

"What?"

Liberty shook her head. "Uh, nothing." She paused. "Do you think there could really be something *else* going on?"

Dane rubbed the stubble on his jaw. "The guy we arrested is clearly low level, so it isn't too far of a stretch to think he's being directed by someone else, given the email account. We need to find out who that person is."

Tate shook his head. "I'll bet Braden knows."

"That's why we should let him go," Liberty said. "He could lead us to them."

"That's a big stretch, Lib." He looked almost sad. "Braden isn't going to play alone. He'll warn them, and then whoever it is could go to ground and never surface again. Or Braden will just spin his wheels, and we'll be watching him for weeks."

Liberty sighed. "I could—"

"No."

Locke said, "Do you think you could convince him to help us, Liberty?"

She looked at Dane. "He's facing charges, right?" When Dane nodded, she said, "Can we offer him a deal? Immunity in exchange for information on who it is and whether there's a bigger plan in play?"

Dane said, "I can talk to the district attorney." He glanced at Locke, and then Tate. "It's worth asking the question. If Braden is worried about blowback, then maybe we can convince them to add witness protection to the deal."

She wanted Tate to be okay with the plan rather than just resigned to it. "It's a good idea."

Tate looked at her. "I'll be working on others, and hopefully something will yield a result."

It wasn't much, but she figured it was the best she'd get. As long as Braden cooperated, they might be able to get all the answers to their questions. Then Tate would see it had been a good idea.

The door flung open. Alana appeared in the doorway, flushed. "Braden got out of his cuffs. He beat up the agent who was watching him and escaped!"

They all stood up. Tate wobbled and set his hands on the table. She wanted to help him but held back so he didn't think she was babying him. Dane looked ready to jump across the table and catch him.

"Braden escaped?"

Locke talked over Alana. "Is Patrick okay?"

"He was just knocked out."

Relief flooded over Locke's face. "Good. We don't need any more injuries, and his getting hurt certainly wasn't part of the plan."

Liberty swung around. "What did you say?"

Tate's voice was hard when he asked, "You let my brother escape on purpose?"

Locke lifted both hands and shrugged. "Whoops."

# SEVENTEEN

"Are you kidding me?" Tate couldn't believe this. Locke had actually *planned* to let Braden go? "At least tell me you have a man on him, following him wherever he goes?"

"GPS tracking device," Locke said, with no remorse on his face for what he'd done. "Plus a man following at a distance. The tracker is just insurance in case we lose him."

Tate shook his head while Locke pulled out his laptop and logged in. He brought up a map, and after a second an orange dot popped up on-screen. "There he is," Locke said.

"No deal?"

Locke shrugged. "If Braden thinks he got away from us, then we get an honest response. We see his real motives, whether that's helping them succeed or bringing you down. Or both."

Tate figured he knew which it was. "We should head out and follow him." He didn't wait for agreement, or permission. He wasn't a Secret Service agent, so he didn't need Locke to tell him to go ahead.

Dane folded his arms. "I lent you guys my truck. You destroyed it."

Instead it was Locke who tossed Tate a set of keys.

Liberty held out her hand for the keys, and he dropped them in her palm. "Concussion plus driving equals no." The look in her eyes was soft.

"I could do it." Tate figured they needed to talk—or at least, he had some things to say—and he didn't need her team to hear them.

As they made their way to the vehicle, he said, "Thank you for driving." Truth was, he probably wasn't up to it.

She looked at him ruefully. "I didn't think you'd say that, of all things. But you're welcome." The smile was genuine, if tired at the edges. "You let me rest earlier. I figured I'd return the favor."

"I appreciate it." He took another pill and swallowed down half the bottle of water. "Seriously, I do." There was so much more to say, but he was exhausted.

Tate awoke when the car engine shut off. He pushed aside the edges of fogginess from sleep and looked across the street. "This the place?"

It was nothing but a closed-down old flooring store, still listed in the phone book last time he'd checked. Because, yes, he still used the phone book. How else was he supposed to find vendors for materials he needed? That and word of mouth were the internet of navigating a small town. Liberty wouldn't understand, so he didn't explain it. He doubted she could survive here.

Still, he asked, "What do you think of my town?"

"For vacation, or to live in?"

Tate shrugged, like there wasn't a world of difference between the two things.

"It's nice. I'd have to see it when it's not all covered

under piles of snow, but there's a certain charm." She smiled. "And what's with the hospital? I wouldn't think there are enough people here to justify a whole hospital."

Tate said, "It serves three counties, but it was built because this movie star moved to a ranch just outside of town. He donated money to fund the entire construction and then some."

"Why?"

"Word is he has severe hemophilia. He wanted doctors and treatment—a whole surgical wing—close by in case there's an accident and he's bleeding internally."

"Wow, it must be serious."

"It can be."

"Do you know him?"

Tate laughed. "I've done some work for him. When he has friends visit and they need added security, he'll pull from local law enforcement. He's actually looking for a permanent security detail, but I'm still considering it. I'm not sure I want to do the work full-time. It's a lot of traveling."

"Oh." Something in her gaze looked a whole lot like a spark of hope. Because he might be getting a job? Tate must not be much of a catch if she was just excited he might be gainfully employed.

He pushed aside the disappointment and said, "So where's Braden?" It was dark outside now, and there wasn't much to see under the yellow glow of streetlamps. The truck smelled like cheeseburgers, and he realized why when she handed over a bag of greasy food.

"Inside the building. We can't get closer, so don't ask."

Tate shot her a look and took a bite.

"Dane told me, in no uncertain terms, not to let you

get involved beyond staking out your brother. We have backup close by, and he said it was up to me to make sure he didn't lose his best deputy."

Tate felt his eyebrows lift. "He said that?"

Liberty nodded.

"Huh."

"I didn't doubt it for a second. You're extremely dedicated, no matter if you're remodeling a bathroom, protecting the president or bringing the law to a small Montana town. Maybe even if you're on protection detail for a movie star."

Tate laughed.

"Although I think the remodel might be a teensy bit of a waste of your abilities." She dropped her hand where she'd held her finger and thumb an inch apart, and took a sip of her gallon-sized drink. "The movie star job is a better fit, I think. But it's not my decision."

Everything in him stilled, and he worked not to show it. "I couldn't do the protection job on my own," he said very carefully. "I would need a team."

Liberty stared at him. "We're supposed to be watching the building." The words came out a whisper.

"Let me worry about Braden. If he slips out of this door and for some reason we don't see, GPS will tell us where he went." Why didn't she want to have this conversation? "There are plenty of people here watching Braden, right?"

Liberty swallowed. Nodded.

"You could work with me, Liberty."

"That's a huge stretch from being broken up, Tate."

He didn't smile, though a tiny part of him wanted to. He knew this was irrational, but love was never clearheaded. "I know that. And despite the fact that the past couple of days have been crazy, it's clear to me things between us haven't changed much. Even though we haven't seen each other for a year, I know now I feel the same as I always did. That never went away." He paused. "Tell me you haven't thought the same."

"I can't tell you that." Liberty shook her head and looked out her window. "It would be a lie."

Tate said, "If you still care about me, and I still care about you, doesn't that leave us in a place where we should at least try to work things out?"

"By me quitting the Secret Service and moving across the country?"

That wasn't the part he wanted to talk about. Still, he said, "If you want me to move back to the East Coast, I would do it."

She turned back to him then, her eyes wide. "You would?"

"I've always known you were worth it, Lib. That was never in question." He sighed. "We had something good between us, something special, and I want to know why you threw it away. Why you threw *us* away."

His attention was half on the building's front door, watching to see when Braden came out, and half on Liberty and the conversation they were having. But he saw the tear that ran down her cheek.

She didn't move to swipe it away. She just stared at him as though he'd pulled the foundation out from under her world. And maybe he had. Maybe the thing that had come between them was so big, it had rocked her to her very core. He'd always thought it had to have been something huge. Liberty didn't make rash, emotional decisions. Despite her crying and then yelling at him that it was over, she'd stood her ground enough he knew she'd made up her mind, and there had been no changing it. That was what had made him so mad.

His head throbbed but he ignored it. This was probably the most important conversation he and Liberty were ever going to have. There was no way he would let an injury come between him and the answer he'd been wanting on for a year.

"Tell me why, Lib."

She sniffed but didn't move. Didn't say anything.

Her phone rang.

"Leave it."

She shifted and pulled it from her jacket pocket. "It's Locke." Liberty answered it, putting the call on speaker. "Yes, Locke?"

Tate gritted his teeth to keep from throwing the offending phone out the window.

"I just got a call from the hospital." Locke's voice was crackly through the phone. "Agent Bearn. Francis." The director cleared his throat. "He didn't make it through surgery. They tried to revive him, but there wasn't much they could do. His injuries were too extensive."

"Okay, thanks for letting us know." Liberty said the words deadpan, looking crushed while Tate's mind was a million miles away from this conversation. Was she going to claim she still couldn't tell him what had caused her to tear both of their lives apart?

"It's been a seriously long day." Locke sighed. "But I'll keep you posted if Braden moves."

Liberty hung up.

Tate said, "Tell me why, Lib."

"I had a good reason." *God, I actually want to tell him.* So why couldn't she just come out and say it? That time in her life had been so painful, and she didn't relish the idea of reliving it. But Tate deserved to know.

"And as much as the reason still stands, I can see us together. Which is crazy," she said. "But you're right, since I got to Montana I see us as a team. It wasn't why I came here." She thought for a second. "I wanted to help you, but maybe I also wanted to see that you were in as much pain as I was… That blog." A sob worked its way up to her throat. "It was so horrible. Everything I thought you wanted to say to the Secret Service. To me."

"Lib."

"It was awful, Tate, and I thought it was you." She tried to collect herself. "Whether it turns out it was Braden or not, it hurt."

Tate reached over and slid his hand on the back of her neck. "I'm sorry for what he said."

"But you do think that. You think I wanted to hurt you, and that's why we broke up, or that you weren't worth me keeping you forever. He said so in the blog, and it's true. Isn't it?"

He didn't nod, but she knew.

"I wanted to be with you forever. And I wanted to give you *everything*. But that meant I had to let you go." She shook her head. "The number of times we talked about it. Working together somewhere, life after the Secret Service. Us. Kids." Her voice broke on that last word.

"We did say that, didn't we?" His tone was measured. So careful. There was so much tenderness in his voice, and there was no way she deserved it.

More tears escaped. Where Tate was, there would always be tears. At least that was how she felt. "I knew how much you wanted kids." She sucked in a breath.

"And it wasn't even that something happened. Just a routine checkup. Oh, by the way, you have this medical condition. You'll probably never be able to have children. The chance of it happening is so minor you may as well consider it nil."

She couldn't stop. The words were flowing now, and if she broke off then she would never be able to finish. "I knew how much you wanted them—how much *we* wanted them. I would never be able to give you that, while someone else would."

Liberty looked at him then. His eyes flashed, wet with unshed tears. Movement out of the corner of her eye caught her attention. She looked over at the building. "Braden's leaving."

*Thank You, God, for something else to concentrate on.* He hadn't given her much, and it honestly felt like He'd taken more from her than He'd ever gifted, but God was still good.

Her struggles didn't change His inherent goodness or His grace in sending His Son for her. Why hadn't she remembered that? As she drove after Braden's car, Liberty realized she'd ignored Him for a year while she licked her wounds. She'd turned her back on God instead of letting Him minister to her and be what she'd desperately needed with Tate no longer in her life.

*I'm so sorry, Lord.* She should never have done that. It wasn't how love acted. And she did love God. She'd just put herself and her own hurt feelings above Him in her life.

A sense of peace flooded her.

*Thank You, God.* He was there with the riches of His grace, ready to extend comfort and hope even now. *Are Tate and I going to find our way back to each other again?* She desperately wanted to know if God's plan included that. After all, what had been the point of the last year? Liberty had grown stronger, forced to weather this all on her own. What if it was so she could go into a marriage with Tate on the firm foundation God had given her?

Maybe that had been His plan, even while she tried to figure her life out on her own.

"Liberty."

She glanced at the passenger seat where Tate wiped his eyes. He pulled up his sleeve and used the material to soak up the emotion. "I'm sorry, Tate."

She didn't want to admit that she should have told him, because she wasn't convinced it was true. If he'd never asked, she wouldn't have. And nothing had really changed. There was still this gulf of what they would never have between them.

Braden turned a corner that led to the center of town, and she followed him a few cars behind in the flow of traffic. If she had told Tate about her diagnosis a year ago, he'd probably have said it was no big deal. But the idea he might settle for something less than what he should have had hurt the most.

"I'm not sorry," he said as she drove. "Okay, maybe I'm sorry that I reacted the way I did to you breaking up with me."

She shook her head and took a left turn. "No, don't say that. I broke your heart, Tate. You were upset, and mad, and you had every right to be. I don't blame you and you shouldn't have to apologize."

"So where does that leave us? I can't say I don't want you to come here and work with me. That would be a lie."

And so they had journeyed full circle back to where they'd been a year ago. Liberty's heart wanted to break all over again, but there weren't any pieces left to shatter. She was going to have to tell him *again* that it wasn't going to work. She couldn't be who he needed her to be.

"Tate…" She hardly knew what to say.

The car in front braked, and Liberty did the same. If the GPS was right, then they were coming up on a spot where the road split into two right by a big chain store. On the other side of the street was the giant hospital.

They crawled to a stop in the line of traffic. She tried to peer around the car in front to see Braden, but it blocked her view. A car idled to her right, more cars behind both of them. The median in the middle was raised, blocking her in. She'd have to bump over it to get out of this spot and then drive down the center of the road.

There was nothing to do but talk.

"It really has been good to see you the past couple of days, despite the craziness and both of us getting hurt. I'm not going to regret coming here."

"But…"

She glanced at him. He was right; there was more. "But I still don't see how we could work together without falling in love more. At least, I couldn't. And it would only be even more painful than it was last time when you realize I can't give you everything you want."

"And if I tell you I don't need us to have kids, that I'll be happy with just you and me?"

She shook her head and kept her attention on the van that pulled up beside them on the other side of the raised median. "You say that now, Tate. But I don't want to be the biggest regret of your life."

"And if you already are?"

The pain cut through her like a knife. "I'm sorry." What else was she supposed to say?

"You can fix this, Lib. My biggest regret is how I walked away after you broke things off. But you're the only one who can choose happiness for us going forward."

Men jumped out of the van, guns drawn. She glanced at Tate, but her gaze fell on the window of his door—where more men jumped out of the vehicle stopped on his side.

The butt of a gun was tapped on her door. "Get out!"

# EIGHTEEN

"Do as they say." Tate's warning was met with a nod from Liberty. She didn't like it, but she would listen to him.

The man beside him cracked open Tate's door. "Let me see your weapon."

Tate pulled the gun he was carrying from the glove box. He handed it over with his other hand raised. There was no sense in fighting these guys. He and Liberty couldn't take four men—that he could see—without getting shot in the process. Not when they already had enough injuries between the two of them.

The man passed Tate's weapon to a guy behind him, and then tugged on Tate's arm. "Get out."

He moved slowly, which was fine because moving at all hurt. Sitting had been nice. The guy didn't need to think he was too agile. He wouldn't try as hard if he thought Tate couldn't fight back.

Tate cleared the door frame and stared the men down like an injured man who had no fight left. He wanted to look at the line of cars behind them. Surely someone was on their phone, calling 911. It was a risky move, taking them in public. And where was Locke? Surely he was in one of these vehicles, or had he been tailing Braden closer than Liberty and Tate? He could've been in front of them. Gone now.

*Help us, Lord.*

"You don't look so good, man." They walked him around the car to where Liberty stood beside a guy who was at least six foot two. He had his hand around her upper arm—her good arm, thankfully.

He looked for tattoos, thinking these guys might be more Russians, but couldn't see any. It didn't mean they weren't affiliated, though. Liberty looked scared out of her mind, making her appear almost helpless when he knew she was anything but. Likely most of the emotion was residual from the conversation they'd been having. He was only glad it served their cause.

*I'll never be able to have children.* And she'd given him up so he could have that family he'd always wanted—without her.

He'd barely seen the strength Liberty had inside her when they were together. He'd had no clue she was courageous enough to let him go. Would he have done the same thing? Tate would've liked to say yes, he'd have let her go to live her life, but maybe he was just too selfish, because Tate didn't think he could've ever let her go.

The barrel of a gun pressed into his spine. Tate started walking, his hands raised. "Wanna tell me where you're taking us?" He asked the question over his shoulder, half not even expecting a reply. They could have simply shot Liberty and Tate in their car, but instead got them out and were now transporting them elsewhere. Still, he was glad they were wanted alive, because he and Liberty still had plenty to talk about.

Tate and Liberty were shoved into the back of the

van, and silver tape was wrapped around their wrists. Tate made sure he kept a gap between his wrists as they were tied in front of him, and glanced over at Liberty to see she had done the same.

The van set off, and they all jerked with the motion.

"I kind of thought you'd put up a fight." The one who'd taken his gun studied Tate, almost like he was disappointed. "But you didn't."

"Sorry I ruined your evening, but I don't plan on getting shot in the street."

The man glanced at Liberty. He touched her cheek. "I can see why you keep this one around."

She turned her face away from the man's hand.

Tate said, "Don't touch her."

The gunman glanced at him. "I get paid to do what I want."

"You're not taking orders?"

"I deliver. That's good enough." He shifted closer to Liberty. "How about you, darlin'? What do you do?"

Tate said, "You have anything to say, you say it to me."

The man smirked. "That's cute, cupcake. But she's cuter."

Tate looked out the front windshield but didn't know which tree-lined road around town this was. Where were they being taken? He worked at the tape, even though he could break it faster with one swift motion, easier than those zip ties the last guys had tied them up with. That would be too noticeable right now, though.

These guys seemed to enjoy the rush of the capture. Maybe they were hoping Tate and Liberty would try to get away so they could hunt them down and catch them again before they turned them over to whoever had paid them. Maybe they did stuff like this for the rush.

When the van made the next turn, Tate's eyes widened. "We're going to my house?"

"We're going to the address they gave us," the gunman said. "What do I care whose house it is?"

Were the dogs here? Tate couldn't remember what Dane had said he'd do with Gem and Joey after he picked Tate up from the hospital, and they wound up taking Braden to the sheriff's office.

Probably he'd put them in the K-9 kennels. If they were here, though, they would be immensely helpful in taking down these guys. He didn't relish the idea that his dogs might get hurt, but they were trained in protection.

They pulled up on the snow-covered front drive, and the man closest to the door slid it open. Liberty shivered. Tate's Christmas lights had been turned off, but the porch light was on. The men held their weapons ready as Liberty and Tate were hauled from the van. They walked them to the barn.

"Inside."

Tate didn't argue, but he had weapons in the house if he could figure out a way to get to them. The barn had a few dog agility items and a bunch of indestructible toys Joey loved. The smell of dog hit him, and he felt the pang. He missed his buddies. They'd been his companions the last year, a gift from God to get him through the days of aching loneliness without Liberty in his life. *I know I've said it before, but thank You.* It was worth saying again now.

Tate was shoved to the far corner.

"Sit."

Liberty was told to sit as well, and she did so right beside him. Close enough her good shoulder touched his.

Tate's head pounded. Not just under the bandage, but also from the realization that Liberty hadn't given up on him because he wasn't worth keeping. He'd thought for so long it was only God who considered him worth anything. It was hard to let go of the belief that the woman he'd loved had thought him dispensable. He thought she'd given him up because he hadn't measured up, when the reality was otherwise. Liberty was the one who thought *she* wasn't worth it in their relationship.

Tate leaned over and kissed the top of her head. His heart broke that she'd thought being unable to get pregnant meant she wasn't worthy of his love and their marriage. They could be happy together. So happy. But she thought he deserved better.

And she couldn't have been farther from the truth.

One of the gunmen walked in the door. "They're fifteen minutes out."

The man who'd been talking to them earlier nodded. "Good." He turned to Liberty. "Means we have time for some fun."

Tate moved so he was covering her with his body. The man closed in and brought his gun down on Tate. He shifted at the last second so it glanced off his shoulder. The impact hit and he cried out. It felt like his shoulder had been shattered.

Liberty was hauled to her feet. "Let me go!"

The man dragged her across the room.

"Lib!" Tate called out, but it didn't help. He couldn't go to her. He could hardly see.

He heard her grunt, then cry out in pain. Then a thud. "Ow!" The man called her a foul name.

Tate climbed to his feet, swaying. He had to help her.

\* \* \*

Liberty kicked out at the man, using the distraction of a fight to snap the tape on her hands. Her shoulder might be hurt, but there was nothing wrong with her legs. He grunted and fell to the floor while his buddies looked on, laughing.

"Guess you met your match," one of them said.

Tate was about to fall over, so she went back to him and they both sat down together. She wasn't going to stay anywhere near that awful guy again.

The men ribbed each other, apparently content to ignore her and Tate, which she thanked God for. They hadn't noticed she was free of her tape. She wanted to stay strong, which was way preferable to dissolving into scared tears.

She'd already cried enough today.

A car pulled up outside. Maybe more than one. Doors slammed, and she could hear the crunch on snow of people approaching. Tate was still beside her, ready for what was about to happen. Liberty wanted to hold his hand, but settled for her arm against his as she worked at the tape on his wrists. It was as close as she could get without sitting on his lap, which would have been very nice. She'd always loved having his arms around her.

Liberty didn't move, though, because neither of them could afford to get too close. Leaning on each other led straight to relying on each other, which led to trust… which ended with her never leaving because she couldn't imagine her life without him.

Exhaustion weighed down her body. At this point she would have paid money for a clean bed—maybe in a nice hotel room—and a solid fourteen hours of complete quiet. Maybe God could help with that—after He got them out of this.

The door opened and a bunch of men walked in. The tape on Tate's hands ripped all the way, and he lowered them to his lap so no one noticed.

A couple of the men who entered she recognized from when they'd kidnapped her and Tate at the mine. Braden was in the middle of the group, not looking happy. She felt Tate's reaction to seeing his brother with them. But maybe he wasn't here because he wanted to be. She still couldn't believe he would do this to a brother who loved him.

The lead guy said, "Where's the boss?"

The group of Russians and Braden parted, and a woman entered, wearing tight black jeans, a turtleneck sweater, four gold rings on her hands and a long unbuttoned coat with fur around the hood.

Liberty gaped. "Natalie."

Tate turned his head to her and said, "I think this is Natalia Standovich."

Liberty figured he was right. She didn't look like the woman with the small child they'd interviewed at home, who didn't know where her loser boyfriend was. This woman was the powerful head of a group of Russians who'd sent federal agents on a manhunt across four counties.

But why?

"Good," she said. "Everything is in place, then." More of an accent came through than she'd had before, completing the transformation of this woman from single mom back into Russian powerhouse.

Liberty tried to wrap her head around all of this. She hadn't thought Braden was any kind of mastermind, but neither could she imagine this woman calling the shots. Clearly Liberty had underestimated her.

"My part is done." The gunman Liberty had kicked started for the door.

Natalia nodded. "You'll be paid."

Each of the guys who had kidnapped her and Tate followed him out the door. Liberty was scared to think about what was going to happen next. *God, help us.* Where was Locke? Surely they'd seen what happened and would follow Braden's GPS to get here and find them.

"Why?" Tate's one-word question startled her.

Natalia shrugged. "As though I have time to explain all that to you. I'm a busy woman."

"I'm sure you are," he said. "But I want to know before I die. Why pin all this on me? Why draw teams of federal agents to this area? I know it's a smoke screen, but it seems risky to me. What is worth you doing all that?"

"You think I would bring them all exactly where I don't want to be seen?" She smiled. "You must not credit me with much intelligence, Mr. Almers. My plan is sound." Natalia lifted her wrist and looked at the face of a huge watch, much bigger than she needed. She noticed Tate's attention was still on her. "You like?"

Liberty gaped. Was she *flirting* with Tate?

Natalia sauntered over and crouched to show him the watch. "It belonged to my father," she said. "Now it's all I have left of him, since I got rid of the other evidence." Her smile was pure evil. She reached up and brushed hair off Tate's forehead.

Seriously?

Liberty didn't exactly want to get into a knockdown,

drag-out fight with this woman, but she clearly thought she could do whatever she wanted. Kind of like the gunman had, and Tate fought the idea every step of the way. His reaction was probably a lot like the feeling surging up in her right now.

Tate jerked his head away from her touch, and she laughed.

Liberty bit her lips together because the alternative was telling the woman to get her hands off him. "So, what now? You kill us and then do whatever it is you have planned?"

Natalia looked at Liberty as though she'd forgotten she was even there.

"We know the plane was just a distraction," Liberty said. "Still, it's kind of overkill, don't you think? A big splash, big headlines, big investigation. Search-and-rescue people. You probably got all the law enforcement personnel in the whole area in one spot looking for the plane."

"And yet you found it." She smiled, like she was proud of them.

"Not before you tried to frame Tate." Liberty's feelings were clear in her tone. "So what I want to know is what's such a big deal you needed a distraction of that magnitude just to get the cops to look the other way?"

Natalia's lips curled up. "Such a smart girl."

Maybe, but it wasn't Liberty who figured it out. It had been Tate. But she didn't explain that—she just wanted Natalia to tell them what it was.

Instead, Natalia stood. She stared down at them in silence for a cool minute.

Uh-oh. That wasn't good. Liberty figured she wasn't going to like whatever happened next.

Natalia pulled a gun from the back of her waistband and held it out. "Braden."

He stumbled, but caught himself as he walked over. His face paled, and his breathing was coming hard—white puffs in the cold barn. Natalia didn't even look at him.

"Braden, shoot them both."

# NINETEEN

Tate stared at his brother. Was Braden going to do it? Would he shoot Tate in his own barn? That might be the end to this. If Locke was going to get here—if the GPS on Braden was working and hadn't been discovered—then he would have been here already. That was how Tate knew the feds and the cops probably weren't coming. He and Liberty were going to have to figure out for themselves how to get out of this, because the alternative was getting killed.

Braden didn't take the gun. Instead, he grinned at Natalia and said, "Babe. You know I don't like blood."

"Yeah, I know." Natalia didn't look sympathetic or impressed by his humor. Her face was impassive, her tone completely neutral. "And I should also know I can't count on you to do anything useful."

"Seems like I did one thing, or you wouldn't have Tasha." That didn't get a reaction either, though Braden thought he was funny. He kept going. "So I guess I'm not completely useless after all." He folded his arms, a smug smile on his face.

Tate tried to figure out what on earth was driving his brother to play the situation this way. Braden wasn't going to achieve anything other than making Natalia mad—which was happening perfectly, considering the tips of her ears were now red.

She moved closer to Braden. "If you want your daughter to know her father past her second birthday—" her tone was low, lethal "—then you pull the trigger and make this problem disappear." She motioned toward Liberty and Tate with the gun. Liberty flinched and huddled against him.

Natalia said, "Because it seems to me like involving your brother, and now his Secret Service girlfriend, was *your* idea."

"It was good. You said you needed a distraction, so I gave you a federal manhunt."

"The downed plane and the missing people were the distraction. The videos, one better. Writing the blog and framing your brother did nothing but leave us in a corner, floundering to fix your mess. The fallout from your plan. While mine had none."

Braden swallowed.

"Since it's your mess, and we have yet to finish this job…" Natalia held up the gun. "Kill them now, and end this ridiculous attempt to improve your station."

He took the gun.

Tate's arm tightened around Liberty. There was no point pretending anymore that they weren't free of their tape. His brother was really going to do it. He was going to kill the two of them because this woman asked him to.

Tate bit the inside of his cheek so hard he tasted blood.

Outside, a car pulled up. Natalia huffed out a breath. "I thought we were going to be done with this before the Venezuelans got here."

That made Tate sit up. The ransom videos had asked

for the release of a Venezuelan. He'd thought it could be a misdirect so the feds would be caught up in paperwork and not as many agents would be focused on finding the missing people. But if the Venezuelans were doing a deal with the Russians, Tate needed to find out what it was. He needed to know why they were here, in case it was the reason the pilot was bribed and those people taken hostage.

He'd been right. About his brother. About all this being a distraction. It wasn't a comfort, though, not when he needed more answers still.

Natalia set her hands on her hips. "Finish them, Braden." She didn't try to lay on the charm like some women did to get their way. No, Natalia Standovich was 100 percent authority, even as she strode out of his barn.

Tate glanced at the shelves, the little cupboard underneath where he kept the radio. He didn't use it often. If he was on call, then the shortwave radio was how the sheriff's office contacted him, and he would stay in the house on those nights. Or use the handheld unit. But there was a radio in here, one he could use to get on the police band.

It was the only way they could get help.

No one stayed behind with Braden. His brother didn't look exactly happy as he stared down Tate. Still, his joking demeanor had disappeared.

"I guess this is the end." Tate's voice came out entirely more grave than he'd have liked.

"It's not like I want to do this." Braden pulled out a phone with his free hand.

"You might not be able to use that. There's no signal up here. The GPS we planted on you is probably not transmitting."

"Natalia found that when we were in town," Braden said. "Cuffed me across the face." He turned his head slightly to show the reddening bruise on his cheek. Braden pocketed his phone, silent for a second before he said, "I've lost my way, Tate."

"You think I don't know that?"

"I think you don't know much of anything about me."

"Druggie. Moocher." Okay, so these weren't compassionate words, or even helpful ones, but the man was about to kill him. Couldn't Tate say whatever he wanted instead of having to forgive right now? His brother didn't need grace or Tate's love, because he was going to carry out that woman's orders regardless.

"What is it, Braden?" Evidently Liberty saw something different.

Braden glanced at her. "I'm sorry I hurt you more than you already were."

"Thank you." Liberty said the words quietly. So quietly they were almost painful to listen to.

Braden frowned, then glanced at the barn door everyone had disappeared through. Looked at Tate. "I'm DEA."

"What?"

Liberty gasped.

Braden said, "I was given an undercover assignment." He blew out a breath. "Eighteen months ago now. Get close to the Russians, report back with intel. It was all going fine until Tasha. That was a onetime thing, not planned, not repeated. I slipped, got too close to Natalia. Now I have a daughter." He sighed. "Everything changed when she was born."

"So you've turned?"

Braden flinched. "I would never do that. But I can't bring down the Russians and keep my daughter safe when the person I'm trying to keep her safe from is her *mother*."

"And you decided to make it so I was framed and imprisoned?"

"I needed you to see me. I needed you to help me get out of this, so I dragged you far enough into it that you couldn't ignore me." Braden ran a hand through his hair. "I knew it would be hard. It's not like you ever do anything wrong. Or need anyone's help. But I managed it."

Tate said, "Give me the gun."

"So you can kill me instead?"

"Just do it."

Braden handed it over reluctantly. Tate fired two shots into the ground. "That'll buy us a few more seconds, and save us from whoever she was going to send in to ask why you didn't do it yet."

"Maybe, but now she's going to send someone to get me because it's done."

Tate shifted and got up. "I'd better move fast, then." He opened the cupboard and turned the knob on the unit, keeping it low, and listened to the dispatcher talk about cows on the wrong side of a fence.

Tate butted in, explaining as fast as he could what was going on and requested all the backup he could get. He said he had DEA agent Braden Almers with him. He could hardly process the fact that his brother was a fed. It explained a lot, even while it contradicted everything Tate had ever believed.

"Copy that, Deputy. Help is on its way."

Tate breathed a sigh of relief and sat back on the floor. "We just have to stay alive until they get here."

Liberty shot him a look. "That's going to be easier said than done."

Liberty strode to the barn door, feeling every one of her aches and pains of the past two days. She opened it a tiny bit to peer out. She had no recourse if they tried anything, not when they had guns and she didn't. Liberty would likely be dead in seconds. Still, she wasn't going to sit around and wait for help while trying not to die.

Tate hissed something, probably for her to get away from the door, but she waved him off. Outside the Russians stood around a shiny Cadillac SUV. A dark-haired man in a cream suit talked to Natalia.

Liberty tried to listen, but all she could hear was the swirl of winter wind whistling in her ears. She couldn't hear anything they were saying, but the conversation didn't look happy.

She turned back to Braden. The DEA agent. Liberty certainly hadn't seen that one coming. A man who'd lost his way and ended up tied up with the wrong people's business? That she could see. The fact that he'd started down that road with the best of intentions was both honorable and the saddest story she'd ever heard.

She needed to know what he knew.

"What made you join a federal agency?"

Braden looked over at her. He knew what she was doing, and it wasn't just a friendly chat between two people who would've been related except for a medical diagnosis.

Tate had sat down again, not looking well at all. This day had been harder on him than anyone, especially given the fact that she'd actually told him why she'd broken up with him. Hopefully now he'd see she was right. And yet, he looked at her with so much promise. Liberty couldn't even think about them—the *them* that might be an *us*—right now.

Braden sighed and sat on an upturned barrel. "Tate had just finished with the army, and he was joining the Secret Service. I was floating around doing odd jobs. Mostly transport. One day I do this delivery, and the guy opens a crate before I leave. It's all AK-47s. The place suddenly swarms with cops and I spend two days answering questions. It turned out I'd been hired to transport them by the DEA, if you'll believe it. They needed some no-name who wasn't connected to bring down this weapons dealer.

"They paid me for the job and about a month later called me again. Asked if I was up for another job. Over the next year it got pretty regular. Take this over here. Do a pick-up for this guy, but let us look at it before you drop it off, because we want to know what he's selling." Braden's gaze had gone dark, as though he had seen things he wished he hadn't.

"There's no record anywhere of me working for the DEA," he continued. "You won't find it, no matter how deep you look. They keep me undercover almost constantly, but the work I do is good. It saves people's lives." He shot Tate a look. "Guess my cover is blown now, though."

"No one is questioning the good you've done, Braden." She needed to say it, because he looked like he needed her to say it. "I'm very proud of you." Liberty shot his brother a look. "And so is Tate, I think."

"Yeah, I am, Bray."

His gaze flicked to his brother, a sheen of tears in his eyes. "But I lost my way, Tate." He looked like a remorseful little boy. "And I don't know if I can get back."

"You have to." Tate stood. "Because you need to go out there and act like we're dead."

Braden cleared his throat. He nodded.

Tate got up and pulled his brother into a hug. "I'm proud of you." He paused. "Tasha is beautiful."

Braden's face twisted, and tears ran down his cheeks. Liberty wasn't going to say it out loud, but that visible emotion would make his story about having killed them more believable. It might even buy them time to wait for rescue.

"Go now, okay?"

Braden nodded, and his gaze locked with his brother's for a long moment. Then he walked out the door.

Tate tilted his head, motioning her over to him. Liberty didn't have the strength to argue. He held out his arms and she walked into them on an exhale. His chest was warm under his sweater, and she slid her arms around his back underneath his coat. Tate leaned down and kissed her head.

"Thank you for being here. I don't think I could've done that without you."

She smiled against his sweater. "You're very welcome."

"I can't believe he's DEA. I didn't even think of it. I just assumed he was a loser."

"That's what he needed you to believe, Tate. Because otherwise you'd have asked too many questions."

Tate's arms tightened for a second, making her hiss at the pain in her shoulder. "Sorry."

"We'll be out of here soon."

"You need a doctor."

She looked up, one eyebrow raised. "So do you, honey."

Tate was quiet for a moment, and then said, "You haven't called me that in a long time."

"I know."

She wanted to tell him she would stay. She wanted to, so badly, but he was the one who needed to be okay with the fact that they would never have children. If he wasn't, Liberty didn't know how she would ever get over him. It would take more than another year for her to grieve seeing him again, knowing all the feelings between them were still there.

"Liberty." He shifted and took hold of her cheeks in the soft way he had with her and no one else.

She nodded beneath his touch. "I know."

The door swung open and hit the wall of the barn.

They both turned around to find Natalia standing there, gun raised.

"I see," she said. And then glanced back over her shoulder. "Kill him."

Tate lunged forward. "No!"

Natalia squared her aim, and Liberty saw it coming. Tate was right in the line of fire.

Natalia fired, but Liberty was already moving. She grabbed Tate and twisted him, swinging him to the side in midair.

The bullet hit her side, almost to her back.

They hit the ground.

Tate rolled, but Liberty couldn't move. She couldn't breathe.

"Police, freeze!"

"Drop the gun! I said, drop it!"

"Hands up."

"Federal agents!"

Liberty blinked and looked up at the ceiling, cobwebs in the corners. Her chest hitched with every breath as her body fought against the pain of movement.

Tate's face came into view. "Liberty." Tears rolled down his cheeks. "Why did you do that?"

She fought for breath, but it hurt. It hurt *so* badly.

"No, no. Just hold on, okay? We'll get you out of here."

"Tate!" Braden was alive?

"Somebody help!" Tate's roar made her flinch. He saw it and touched her cheeks. "Everything is okay, just hold on."

Liberty didn't think everything was okay. But all she could say was, "Missed you."

And then everything went black.

# TWENTY

Tate sat in the chair, ate in the chair and slept in the chair until she woke up. The only break he'd taken was for the doctor to check him out. He'd jarred his head in the fall and then blubbered like a baby in front of basically everyone he knew until the ambulance doors closed.

Then it had been all about work until he could get to the hospital.

He'd almost collapsed when he walked through the door, but Dane had been there to catch him. Tate's name had been cleared, and Dane had given back his badge. It was more of a symbolic move than anything else, but he'd been given back his position again and the respect that came with it.

Now all he needed was for Liberty to wake up.

Tate couldn't believe she'd taken a bullet for him. He was the one who was supposed to have been protecting her, and there she went throwing herself in harm's way to protect him. And it could have killed her. So easily.

He looked at her, lying in that bed. Pale face. Wires. Tubes. The steady beep of her heart on the monitor.

He didn't know whether to throttle her for what she'd done, or just be extremely grateful.

If she let him, Tate intended on spending the rest of his life showing her how grateful he was. They'd proven they were miserable apart. And they'd proven they were a great team together.

Liberty had broken up with him *because* she loved him so much.

And because she loved him that much, Tate was never going to let her go.

Liberty swam to the surface of consciousness. Her body was numb, and not in a way she liked. Breath hissed from her mouth, and she heard someone say, "Uh-oh."

Liberty blinked, and Tate's face swam into view.

"You're mad."

Her thoughts coalesced like puzzle pieces, but she couldn't see the image yet.

"You're going to drive the nurses crazy, aren't you?" That smile. She'd always loved his smile. "Don't worry. I'll make sure everything is good. You just worry about getting better."

He leaned down and kissed her forehead, and Liberty slipped back into sleep.

Tate watched her eyes flutter, and then open. She'd woken up several times, but hadn't spoken yet. Unless he counted the meds-induced babbling that made no sense. Although it had been interesting when she talked about how cute he was.

He smiled to himself as she came to, wondering if

this would be the time he'd be able to tell her everything that had happened since she'd been shot.

"Hey." Her eyes shut for a couple of seconds, then opened again.

"Hey." Tate settled on the side of the bed. "How are you feeling?"

"Weird."

He nodded. "They moved you from ICU to a regular room. You're out of the woods, but it cost you your spleen."

"I never liked that thing anyway."

Tate smiled. "I love you. I'm glad you're back."

"So am I."

He meant more than she probably knew. Not just the fact that she was awake, but that she was back in his life as well.

But he didn't talk about that now. He gave her a drink of water, and the nurse got the doctor. They checked her out. Progression would be slow, but it would be evident. She wasn't supposed to move a lot, or get stressed out. Just rest.

Tate nodded. "I'll make sure she does."

Liberty shot him a look, which he ignored. When the doctor left, she looked at him. He ignored that as well. "Want to hear what has happened?"

She scrunched up her nose, but he could see in her eyes that she wanted to talk about something else.

Tate started in anyway. "Braden explained what the Russians and the Venezuelans had been into. A big deal, monumentally big, actually. The Russians had been hired to safely get a container full of guns and drugs across the border. There was money and diamonds. But it gets worse. When we seized it, in conjunction with the DEA and state police, we found four girls and a boy in there as well. Hidden behind all the stuff." His voice hitched. "Just kids." That had been the hardest part, even given the victory of being able to rescue those missing children and start the process of returning them to their homes.

He went on, "The truck was leaving the country, bound for a plane just over the Canadian border, where the Venezuelans were going to transport all that stuff back home. The ransom demand for their man to be released from prison was supposed to be part of it, and when the feds rounded up everyone at my house, they were seriously mad that hadn't happened. Of course, Natalia didn't care, she just lawyered up and started naming names to get a lighter sentence."

He shook his head. "I'm not sure it's going to happen, when she orchestrated the hijacking of a plane transporting federal employees."

Liberty said, "Wow."

He nodded. "It was a victory for sure, and we have everyone involved. It's going to take the Secret Service, DEA and state police some time to unpack it all, but it's over."

She bit her lip. "What about Braden?"

"Natalia threatened to kill him," Tate said. "He's talking to the US Attorney about a deal to get him and Tasha into witness protection."

"But you'll never see them again."

Tate took her hand and threaded his fingers through hers. "But they'll be safe."

"Tate."

He looked up. "Kids or no kids, I'm not going to let you walk out of my life."

"I can't walk, Tate. I'm in a hospital bed."

He didn't smile. "You know what I mean. We're a great team, and we never stopped loving each other."

"I love you, Tate. That's never changed."

"I'm going to be here until the day they let you go, and then I'm going to take you back to DC. We'll make this work, Lib. Because I can't bear thinking about the alternative. It'll be worse than this past year." He paused. "I love you so much. I want us to be together, and I'll do whatever I have to to make that happen."

"And if I was to resign from the Secret Service and join your private protection team?"

"You want to take the job?"

"I want to be where you are. And you love it here."

He nodded. "I do. But I want to be where you are as well."

"Good." She tugged on his hand with her good one until he leaned down and she lifted her chin. Tate kissed her gently, but for a long time.

"Good." He smiled. "And I had Alana get something for me while you were out." Tate stuck his fingers in his jeans pocket and pulled out the now-warm metal, which had been in his dresser drawer. He held up the engagement ring he'd given her the first time.

"Marry me, Lib. Again."

"Again?" Her lips twitched.

He laughed. "You know what I mean."

"Yes," she said. "I'll marry you *every* time."

"Whatever happens, whatever the future holds," he said, "I don't want to face it without you."

\* \* \* \* \*

Dear Reader,

Thank you so much for journeying with me through the craziness of Tate's and Liberty's lives. So often we feel like we're not worthy, but thank God that He shows us our worth to Him with His amazing gift of grace and forgiveness—and His son.

My prayer for you is that you understand the richness of His love toward you, and open your life to see that love displayed in the many ways God blesses us.

I hope you'll join me for future books! In the meantime, you can check out my other books at www.author-lisaphillips.com and contact me there as well. You can also write to me c/o Love Inspired Books, 24th Floor, 195 Broadway, New York, NY 10007.

God bless you richly,
*Lisa*

# Get 2 Free Books,
## Plus 2 Free Gifts—
### just for trying the Reader Service!

LIS17R2

## SPECIAL EXCERPT FROM

*Love Inspired.*
# SUSPENSE

*Special Agent Tanner Wilson has only one clue to figure
out who left a baby at the Houston FBI office—his
ex-girlfriend's name written on a scrap of paper.
But Macy Mills doesn't recognize the little girl that
someone's determined to abduct at any cost.*

*Read on for a sneak preview of
THE BABY ASSIGNMENT by Christy Barritt,
available January 2018 from Love Inspired Suspense!*

Suddenly, Macy stood. "Do you smell that, Tanner?"

Smoke. There was a fire somewhere. Close.

"Go get Addie," he barked. "Now!"

Macy flew up the steps, urgency nipping at her heels.

Where there was smoke, there was fire. Wasn't that
the saying?

Somehow, she instinctively knew that those words
were the truth. Whoever had set this fire had done it on
purpose. They wanted to push Tanner, Macy and Addie
outside. Into harm. Into a trap.

As she climbed higher, she spotted the flames. They
licked the edges of the house, already beginning to
consume it.

Despite the heat around her, ice formed in her gut.

She scooped up Addie, hating to wake the infant when
she was sleeping so peacefully.

Macy had to move fast.

She rushed downstairs, where Tanner waited for her. He grabbed her arm and ushered her toward the door.

Flames licked the walls now, slowly devouring the house. Tanner pulled out his gun and turned toward Macy.

She could hardly breathe. Just then, Addie awoke with a cry.

The poor baby. She had no idea what was going on. She didn't deserve this.

Tanner kept his arm around her and Addie.

"Let's do this," he said. His voice held no room for argument.

He opened the door. Flames licked their way inside.

Macy gasped as the edges of the fire felt dangerously close. She pulled Addie tightly to her chest, determined to protect the baby at all costs.

She held her breath as they slipped outside and rushed to the car. There was no car seat. There hadn't been time.

Instead, Macy continued to hold Addie close to her chest, trying to shield her from any incoming danger or threats. She lifted a quick prayer.

*Please help us.*

As Tanner started the car, a bullet shattered the window.

*Don't miss
THE BABY ASSIGNMENT by Christy Barritt,
available January 2018 wherever
Love Inspired® Suspense books and ebooks are sold.*

www.LoveInspired.com